"You Di[d]..." You Ha[d] My Son."

A tremor shook Selene's lips before she contained it. She wasn't as in control as she'd like him to think.

Next second, Aris thought he might have imagined it as she shrugged, her expression implacable. "Listen, Sarantos, if you're worrying this might have repercussions for you, don't. I wasn't about to check with you to make sure it was okay with you if I had Alex. I'm sure if you'd known, you wouldn't have wanted him. I'm the one who decided to have him. So, he's mine, and mine alone. End of story."

He stood there, stinging from the barrage of harsh truths.

She was right.

If she'd "checked" with him, he would have said a baby was literally the last thing he wanted. Until he'd followed her here and seen Alex, the very idea of having a child had filled him with terror.

But he *had* seen Alex.

And he'd seen *her* again.

How would anything he'd ever believed about himself apply anymore?

Dear Reader,

When I was invited to write for the Billionaires and Babies series, I was thrilled. The scenario came to me almost at once, the most emotionally charged one I could think of. There was nothing more heart-melting for me than to write about a man—powerful and self-sufficient to the point of total detachment—who found himself driven by emotional needs he always believed he didn't possess to become not only a lover and a prospective husband but, as my hero calls it, one part of a parent duet. The melting rate increased when his baby breached all his defenses with one single, six-toothed smile—and when that baby's mother turned out to be the woman he's long craved but whom he always thought would be the last woman on earth to want or accept him.

I adored writing Aris and Selene's story, with all of its twists and turns and escalating emotional stakes. Their journey of self-discovery and reaching out to one another against all odds was one of my most satisfying writing experiences ever. I hope you enjoy reading it!

I love to hear from readers, so please contact me at oliviagates@gmail.com. I'd love it if you find me on Facebook at www.facebook.com/oliviagates and follow me on Twitter at www.twitter.com/OliviaGates.

Please also visit me on the web at www.oliviagates.com to find out about my latest releases, read excerpts from upcoming books and enter my contests.

Enjoy, and thanks for reading.

Olivia Gates

OLIVIA GATES

THE SARANTOS SECRET BABY

Recycling programs
for this product may
not exist in your area.

ISBN-13: 978-0-373-73093-3

THE SARANTOS SECRET BABY

Books by Olivia Gates

Desire

*The Desert Lord's Baby #1872
*The Desert Lord's Bride #1884
*The Desert King #1896
†The Once and Future Prince #1942
†The Prodigal Prince's Seduction #1948
†The Illegitimate King #1954
Billionaire, M.D. #2005
In Too Deep #2025
  "The Sheikh's Bargained Bride"
**To Tame a Sheikh #2050
**To Tempt a Sheikh #2069
The Sarantos Secret Baby #2080

*Throne of Judar
†The Castaldini Crown
**Pride of Zohayd

OLIVIA GATES

has always pursued creative passions like singing and handicrafts. She still does, but only one of her passions grew gratifying enough, consuming enough, to become an ongoing career—writing.

She is most fulfilled when she is creating worlds and conflicts for her characters, then exploring and untangling them bit by bit, sharing her protagonists' every heart-wrenching heartache and hope, their every heart-pounding doubt and trial, until she leads them to an indisputably earned and gloriously satisfying happy ending.

When she's not writing, she is a doctor, a wife to her own alpha male and a mother to one brilliant girl and one demanding Angora cat. Visit Olivia at www.oliviagates.com.

To my mom. May you be well and be with me always.

One

The devil had come to her father's funeral.

Though Selene Louvardis had always heard it would be bad-mouthing the devil to call Aristedes Sarantos that.

Aristedes Sarantos. The destitute nobody who'd risen from the quays of Crete to rocket to household-name status in the shipping industry and beyond. A name that everyone whispered in awe, a presence everyone heeded. A power everyone feared.

Everyone but her father.

For over a decade, since she'd been seventeen, not a week had passed without her hearing about yet another clash in her father's ongoing war with the then twenty-seven-year-old man. The man her father had once said should have been his biggest ally, but who'd become his bitterest enemy.

Now the war was over. Her father was dead. Long live the king. If her brothers didn't put their own differences aside, Aristedes Sarantos would soon assimilate the empire that her father had built and they'd expanded before each had tried to pull it in a different direction. If her brothers couldn't work together, Aristedes would rule supreme.

She'd been shocked to see him at the funeral. They'd arrived to find him there. He'd stood in the distance, dominating the windy New York September day as if he existed outside time and awareness, his black coat flapping around his juggernaut's body like a giant raven—or a trapped, tormented soul. She hadn't thought it strange when someone had speculated that he'd come to claim her father's.

She'd thought he'd leave after the burial. But he'd followed the mourners' procession to her family mansion. For the past minutes, he'd surveyed the scene from the threshold, assessing the situation like a general taking stock of a battlefield, a magician setting his stage by casting a thrall on the crowd.

The moment she thought he'd turn around and leave, Sarantos moved forward.

She held her breath as his advance cut a swath through the crowd. On a physical level, apart from her brothers, who stood his equal, everyone he passed by dwindled into insignificance. On other levels, he was unrivaled.

Her brothers wore their distinction like second skins, and she had heard from the endless women who ricocheted in their orbits how sinfully irresistible they were. To her own senses, they had none of Sarantos's gravity well of influence, of ruthless charisma, of unrepentant danger.

She felt it now like an encroaching wave of darkness, seductive and overpowering and inescapable.

Only her brothers stood their ground at his approach, glaring at him with a decade's worth of pent-up enmity. She feared the youngest of her three older brothers, Damon, would intercept him, kick him out. Or worse. His expression showed him struggling with the impulse before paying

Sarantos what his older brothers had decided his presence here deserved. Pointed disregard.

Suddenly she felt fed up with them all.

No matter what they thought or felt, out of respect for their father, they should have done what he would have. Hektor Louvardis wouldn't have treated anyone who'd come to his turf—including Sarantos, his worst enemy—with such sullen passive aggression.

Just as she decided to tell her oldest brother, Nikolas, to act his part as the new patriarch of the Louvardis family and shake the man's hand and accept his condolences graciously, her lungs emptied.

Said man was zeroing in on *her*.

She froze as his steel-and-silver gaze slammed into hers across the bustling space, holding her prisoner.

Her next scheduled breath wouldn't come. Her mind stuttered to a standstill as the power and purpose of his strides eliminated the gap between them, before it kicked off again in a jumble. She was dimly aware that everyone was openly hanging on his every move like she was, bursting with curiosity and anticipation.

Then he stopped before her and brought the whole world to a halt with him. Made it cease to exist. Made her feel tiny, fragile, when she was anything but.

She stood five-foot-eleven in her two-inch heels, but he still dwarfed her. She'd never realized he was this imposing, this…incredible. And he wasn't even handsome. No, calling him handsome would almost be an insult. He was…one of a kind. Unadulterated power and raw maleness in human form. And she already knew that the unique package housed as formidable a brain, intensifying his appeal. But again, *appeal* was a lame word when describing his impact. Aristedes Sarantos didn't just *appeal* to her. He incited a jarring, helpless, unstoppable response.

She winced inwardly. What a time to revisit the feverish crush she'd had on him since the first time she'd seen him. She'd soon known it was futile, not just because he was her family's enemy, but because he took zero interest in others. She still hadn't been able to stop herself from taking every opportunity to feed her fascination by sneaking as many up-close glimpses of him as possible.

But she'd never been *this* close. Had never had him looking down at her with such focus. She could now see that his eyes were the crystalline manifestation of molten steel, bottomless vortices of—

She gave herself a mental slap.

Stop fluttering over his imperfect perfections like a schoolgirl who's bumped into her rock idol. Say something.

She cleared her throat. "Mr. Sarantos." She extended her hand. "Thank you for coming."

He didn't answer, didn't take her hand. Just stared down at her until she realized it was as if he didn't really see her. She pulled back her suspended hand to her side, her eyes lowering, escaping the embarrassment and the crowd's scrutiny.

"I'm sorry he's gone."

His voice, so low, so dark and fathomless, boomed along her nerves and inside her rib cage like a bone-shaking bass line. But it was his words, their import, that made her gaze flicker up to the unwavering opacity of his own.

Not *I'm sorry for your loss,* the mantra everyone had droned to her for the past hours. He wasn't here to offer her, or any of her family, condolences, real or perfunctory.

Aristedes Sarantos was here for himself. He *was* sorry her father was gone. And she suddenly realized why.

"You'll miss fighting with him, won't you?"

His eyes bored into hers, yet still made her feel as if he

was looking through her into his own realizations. "He made my life…interesting. I'll miss that."

Again, he was focused on what her father's death meant to him. His candidness, his unwillingness to bend to the laws of decorum, to dress his meaning in social acceptability and political correctness, took her breath away. And freed her to admit her own selfishness.

One day, she'd probably think about the loss of her father in terms of having his prolific life aborted at a robust sixty-six, in terms of what the whole family, the whole world, had lost. But she could think of nothing but her own loss now. The gaping void his absence left inside her.

"He made my life…so many things," she whispered. "I'll miss them all."

Again he didn't commiserate.

After a beat he said, "He wasn't ill."

Statement. She nodded, shook her head, felt her throat closing. She had no idea. He hadn't seemed ill. But her father would have never admitted to any weakness, would have hidden it at any cost. He could have been gravely ill, for all they knew.

"And he died shortly after 11:00 a.m. yesterday."

Her father had been found dead in his office at 12:30 p.m. Selene had no idea how Sarantos had found that out.

He went on. "At 9:00 a.m, the head of my legal team was in touch with yours, concerning our complementary bids for the British navy contract." She knew that. She'd been the one his man had talked to. She'd relayed the restrictive, ruthless, nonnegotiable—if in her opinion, ultimately fair and practical—terms to her father by phone. "At eleven, Hektor called me." Selene lurched at the sound of her father's name on his lips. If she didn't know better, she'd say this was how a man uttered a friend's name. More than a friend. "He tore into me, then he hung up. Within the hour he was dead."

Before she could say anything, he gave her a terse nod and turned on his heel.

She gaped after his receding form until he exited the mansion.

Was that *it?* He'd come to say it had been him who'd pushed her father beyond endurance, drove him to his death? *Why?*

But since when did anyone understand why the unfathomable Aristedes Sarantos did anything?

Instead of running after him and demanding an explanation, she could only burn in an inferno of speculation and frustration as the hours dragged on before everyone had pity on her family and left them alone.

She allowed her brothers to wrap up the macabre proceedings and stumbled out of the mansion.

She had to get away. Probably permanently.

She flopped into her car. She'd roam the streets. Maybe tears would come again, relieve the pressure accumulating inside her.

She'd just swung her car outside the gates when she saw him.

It was totally dark, and he stood outside the streetlight's reach, but she recognized him at once.

Aristedes Sarantos. Standing across the street, facing the mansion, like a sentinel on unwavering guard.

Her heart revved from its sluggish despondence into a hammering of confusion, of curiosity. Of excitement.

Why was he still here?

She decided to ask him, that and everything else, made a U-turn. In a minute she brought the car to a stop beside him.

She thought he hadn't noticed her until she opened the passenger window, leaned across and addressed him.

"You came without a car?"

It was a long, still moment before he unfastened his gaze from the mansion and swept it down to her.

He gave an almost imperceptible shrug. "I sent it away. I'll walk back to my hotel."

Before she could think, she unlocked the doors. "Get in."

He stared at her. After another endless moment, he opened the door, lowered his muscled body beside her with all the economy and grace of a leopard settling into an effortless coil.

Electricity skidded across her skin, zapped her muscles. Air disappeared from the night. All from one brush of his shoulder, before he presented her with his profile and went statue-still.

She knew she should ask which hotel, start driving. Do something. She couldn't. Just having him this near was messing up her coherence centers. And that when he seemed not to notice her. How would she feel if he...

Stop it, you moron. You're a twenty-eight-year-old businesswoman and attorney, not some slobbering teenager!

It was him who spoke, to specify which hotel. Then he fell silent again. His silence badgered her with the blunt edge of the emotions it contained, smothered.

Before tonight, she'd thought Aristedes Sarantos had no feelings.

In twenty minutes she pulled in the driveway of one of the five-star-plus hotels he was known to live in. As far as the world knew, the man who could buy a small country had no home.

He opened his door. Just as she thought he'd exit the

car without a look back, he turned to her, snatching the air from her lungs again. His eyes glinted in the dimness with something that shook her, something bleak and terrible.

"Thank you." His voice had dipped an octave lower than usual. After a beat he added, "See you in the battlefield."

He turned then. He would exit the car, and she would never see him again except as the enemy. But before they returned to their battle stations, she had to know.

"Are you okay?" she said, fighting the desire to reach for his hand, to cup his face, to offer him…something.

He stilled, turned back to her. One formidable eyebrow rose. "Are you?"

She inhaled tremulously. "What do you think?"

"But cross-examining me would make you feel better."

A chuckle burst out of nowhere. "I'm that transparent?"

His gaze darkened. "Right now, yes. Shoot."

"Here?"

"If you like. Or you can walk me to my room."

The way he said that, such a manifestation of virility, had another chuckle trembling on her lips. And she discovered it wasn't only her lips that were trembling. She was shaking all over.

He reached for her hand, absorbed its tremors in the steadiness of his. "When was the last time you ate?"

He had a point. This reaction was due to low blood sugar along with everything else. "Yesterday morning."

"That makes two of us. Let's get something to eat."

And for the next half hour, she just let him steer her. He took her up to his presidential suite, ordered a Cordon Bleu dinner, encouraged her to eat by showing her how a meal was supposed to be demolished, systematically, like he did everything.

It felt surreal, having Aristedes Sarantos catering to her needs. Weirder still to be in his suite but to feel no threat of any sort. She didn't know if she should be pleased that he was such a gentleman, or disappointed he could be so much of one around her.

After dinner he took her to the suite's sitting area, served her herbal tea. They hadn't talked much during dinner. She'd been too shaky, and he'd been drifting in and out of his own realm.

He brought his own mug, stood there feet from her, hand in pocket, focus inward. Suddenly he started talking.

"We've had too many confrontations to count, but our last one was different. It wasn't like him. It was a…rant."

He'd brought it back to her father. To what had driven him to crash his funeral. Guilt? Was he capable of feeling it? Her father had been adamant that Aristedes had no human components.

"You think you pushed him too far," she whispered. "Caused his death."

He exhaled, shook his head. "I think he pushed himself too far, in his need never to let me win, or at least to never let me go unpunished for winning."

"You still feel responsible." This was her own statement.

He didn't refute it. "I never understood his enmity. We weren't rivals. We worked in complementary fields. We should have been allies."

"That's what he said…once."

This was news to him. Disturbing news. The bleakness gripping his face deepened. "But he disapproved of me and my origins too much to accept that he could put his hand in mine."

Her gaze, her voice, sharpened. "My father wasn't a snob."

He shrugged, unaffected by her sudden resentment. "He wouldn't have considered it snobbery. Certain things are too deeply engraved in the Greek persona. But you wouldn't know that. You were born here."

"That might mean I'm more American than Greek, but my father remained mostly Greek. I knew him."

"Did you?"

Two simple words. They fell on her with shearing force, stripping away a confidence she could have sworn her life on. And it made her mad.

She sat up to bring him into the searing immediacy of her displeasure. "I wasn't only his daughter, I was his protégée, then his business associate."

"Ne." Suddenly something that felt spiked in danger and molded of darkness and compulsion rolled from his chest. The amusement it transmitted was only vocal, didn't tinge his expression. Accompanying it was the first glance that was all hers, as if he'd suddenly realized she was there. "And a worthy warrior he added to his ranks. I struggled for a way out of those traps you laid in that last set of so-called negotiations."

A wave of heat cascaded through her. She'd been confident she'd had him where they'd wanted him. His own legal team, the best of the best, had been stymied. But not him.

"You eventually found it." She licked her lips, remembering how chagrined she'd felt when he had. How excited. How she'd worked her butt off to place more roadblocks in his way.

The first thing resembling a smile attempted to melt the cruelty of his masterfully sculpted lips. "Not that you just let me walk out of your maze of hurdles."

She almost shuddered as the new heat in his eyes enveloped her, bringing with it the intoxication she'd experienced whenever he'd lobbed her best shots back at her, the exhilaration of dueling with him, even if through long-distance legal swashbuckling. She'd won against him almost as much as she'd lost. Until this last time, when she'd felt he'd finally figured her out, would never lose against her again….

He suddenly put down his mug, straightened to stroll toward her with those languid, goose-bump-raising, purpose-laden strides of his. He didn't stop until his legs almost touched her knees.

The look he gave her now almost made her collapse back on the couch. Hot with appreciation, with challenge. All for *her*.

"You're good. The best who ever tried to trip and shackle me. And you've cost me big. But I'll always win in the end. I have a decade on you in age, and about a century's worth of experience and wiles. Unlike you, I learned the law for one purpose—to find out how to play dirty and come out the other side clean."

She coughed a ridiculing huff. "And you don't understand my father's enmity."

"So I understood. Doesn't mean I accepted it. He should have used my abilities. I complemented him."

"His vision in business clashed with yours diametrically."

"And therefore mine is wrong and evil?"

"You're bent on success, no matter the price."

"That is what business is all about."

"You take 'business is business' to a new realm. That wasn't his way."

"No."

After that monosyllable of resignation and finality, a long silence unfurled.

When it got too heavy, too suffocating, she decided to tackle another bleakness, air another heartache.

"I heard about your brother," she whispered.

His youngest brother had died in a car accident five days ago. She hadn't thought it possible, or even acceptable, for her, the daughter of his enemy, to offer condolences, let alone attend the funeral.

He sat down beside her. His thigh burned hers through the fabric of their pants. His eyes turned into twin lightning storms.

"Are you going to say you're sorry he's gone, too?" he rasped.

She felt the breakers of his pain collide with hers, shook her head. "Beyond a human sorrow for the death of someone so young, there was no personal connection for me to mourn. Not like the one you evidently had—and maybe never realized you had—with my father. I can only give you the same honesty you gave me when you didn't pretend to be sorry for my loss. I can only tell you the one thing I do feel. Sorry for yours."

His arm suddenly clamped around her waist.

Her lungs emptied on a soundless cry of surprise as she slammed against his steel-fleshed body. He gave her a compulsive squeeze and her flesh turned to a pliant medium that melted into his hard angles from breast to hip.

He held her eyes for a tempestuous moment, declaring his intent, demanding her surrender. Then his lips crashed over hers.

He swallowed her cry, poured a growl of hunger inside her, his lips possessing hers, moist, branding, his tongue thrusting deep, over and over, singeing her with pleasure, breaching her with need, draining her of reason.

And it was like a floodgate exploded. She went under in his taste and ferocity and domination. His hands joined in her torment, gliding all over her, never pausing long enough to appease, until she writhed against him, whimpered, begged, not knowing what she was begging for, not knowing what to offer but her surrender.

Pressure built, behind her eyes, in her chest, loins. Her hands convulsed on his arms until he relented, took it to the next level. He freed her blouse from her pants, his hands dipping beneath, feeling like lava against her inflamed skin, undoing her bra, releasing her swollen breasts and a measure of the pressure suddenly about to make her explode.

She keened. With relief, with the spike in arousal. "Please…"

His eyes shot up, twin steel infernos. Everything inside her surged toward him, needing anything…*anything* he'd do to her….

What was she thinking, doing? This was *Aristedes Sarantos.* Her family's enemy. *Her* enemy…

"Say no," he groaned as he sank back over her, suckling her neck in pulls that made her feel he was drawing her heartbeats right into his own body. "Tell me to stop. If you don't tell me to stop, I'll devour you."

The brief shock at the acute turn this had taken was expunged right there and then. She was certain of one thing.

She couldn't say no. She couldn't bear it if he stopped.

And she told him. "I can't. I *won't.*"

"Then tell me not to stop. Tell m—" He stopped, pushed away from her, hissed as if he was tearing his skin off. "*Theos*…I *have* to stop, to tell you to go." When she started to protest, he gritted his teeth. "I don't have protection."

Her heart punched her ribs. With elation, that he didn't have protection as a mandatory measure. With disappointment, that this would force him to put an end to this magical interlude. And she couldn't let it end.

"I'm safe…and i-it's the wrong time of the month…"
She almost choked. She'd only ever had sex with one man,
three times to be exact, years ago. Anyone hearing her
would think she was an old hand in impromptu sexual
encounters.

But she didn't care. She wanted this. Wanted *him*. Felt
she'd disintegrate if he didn't just…just…

"I'm safe, too." He was back over her, giving her what she
needed, with the exact force and urgency that she needed
it.

He tore at her clothes, predatory growls issuing from
him at every inch he exposed and owned. Those became
aggressive with impatience when her pants' zipper snagged
and tore in his urgent fingers.

"Skirts, *kala mou,* wear skirts…"

Her ravenous sobs turned to giddy giggles, seeming to
feed his frenzy. She hadn't worn skirts since high school.
She'd wear anything he wanted, if it made him mindless
with the same need tearing at her.

She writhed with stimulation and embarrassment as he
bared her legs to his hunger, captured them in his powerful
hands, spread them for his bulk and ground his hardness
against her soaked core through their remaining clothing.
She cried out with anticipation…and anxiety.

If she felt her heart would stampede out of her rib cage
now, how would she feel when he took it further, took
her?

Then he slid down on his knees between her legs, feasted
on them, sinking his teeth into her quivering flesh, leaving
marks that evaporated as they formed, yet felt as if they had
marked her forever.

"Beautiful, perfect…" He dragged her panties down her
legs, opened them wide and without giving her a chance to
draw another breath, he opened the lips of her core, slid his

fingers into her fluid heat. She cried out, then again with the first contact of his hot lips and tongue with her swollen, intimate flesh. Then again and again when he licked and suckled her, growling his enjoyment.

She was dying for the release she felt would consume her with his next strokes, but she wanted far more to be joined with him, to reach that release with him, around him.

And she begged, "With you, please…with you filling me…"

He lifted raging eyes to her, rasped something incoherent as if all the tethers holding his sanity in place had snapped wholesale. He rose over her, freed himself, left no chance for the alarm at his daunting size to register before he dragged her by the legs, lifted them around his waist. He caressed her flaming flesh with his satin steel, bathed himself in her flowing readiness in one teasing stroke, from her bud to her opening.

On the next stroke, he plunged inside her, fierce and full.

Her whole body arched before going nerveless as he overstretched her, forged to unknown depths inside her. She collapsed beneath him in sensual shock so deep her sight, her scream, vanished, only one thing left in her. The need to engulf all of him, have him invade her to the last reaches of her body and soul, assuage all the anguish and erase all the loss.

And he did, thrust inside her over and over, thrust her beyond her limits, beyond her endurance, beyond her existence.

She regained her sight, saw him above her, eyes crackling with the same insanity that had her at its mercy. Then her voice came back, begged him for more, more, to never, ever stop.

The begging became shrieks as her insides splintered

on pleasure too sharp to register, then to bear, then to bear having it end. His roars echoed her desperation as his body caught the current of her convulsions, fed them with his own, poured his release on the conflagration that was consuming her, sending it spiraling out of control.

Nothing registered for an eternity.

Nothing but being merged with him in ultimate intimacy, feeling him still shuddering over her, inside her, pouring his essence into her recesses.

Then everything seeped back, a trickle at first, then a current. Then a flood surged over her.

What had she done?

This should be a fantasy of her overwrought psyche. Finding an explosive release in the arms of the one man who would cause enough trouble and heartache to take her mind off her bereavement.

But this was real.

She'd made unbelievable, abrupt, climactic love with Aristedes Sarantos.

And she wanted more.

Aftershocks still quaked through her; his rock-hard arousal still occupied her brutally satisfied flesh. But pangs of withdrawal were already intensifying, tension roaring inside her again. More, her body screamed. Him, them, like this. Like this...

As if he'd heard the clamor, he responded to the intimate flesh throbbing demand around him, thrust deeper into her as he raised himself on extended arms, palms flat beside her head.

She dreaded meeting his eyes.

Would that distance be there again? Or worse, dismay, or disdain or disgust?

"You should not only be a licensed attorney, but a licensed weapon, *kala mou*. You could easily finish a man."

Her gaze fluttered to his and she almost whimpered in relief.

Far from anything she'd feared, his eyes were pouring scorching sensuality and indulgence over her. She felt so thankful that she dug her fingers into the luxury of his mussed satin locks, brought his head down to close each eye with a trembling kiss.

He stilled over her, letting her offer and savor the moment of tenderness.

Then he pulled back. And she gasped.

That dangerous desire was a storm roiling in his eyes again, the drugged veil of short-lived satisfaction vanishing in the blast of renewed need.

Her breath caught as she felt him grow impossibly bigger inside her, arched her back into the couch involuntarily, thrusting her hips to accommodate more of him, croaked, "It doesn't seem like you're…finished."

"I'm far from it. If you know what you're inviting."

"I *want* to know."

He swooped down, fused their lips, his carnal possession perfect in its flavor and ferocity. "Remember, this is you giving me license to take you, to do everything to you."

She clutched him closer still, clenched around him, her lips trembling on a breaker of the urgency that was tossing her into its turbulence. "Yes, everything…take it all, give it to me…"

He reared up, tore open her blouse, then his shirt. Her loosened bra disappeared off her aching breasts, his hair-roughened chest replacing it, inflaming them to agony. He exchanged that torment for his teeth and lips, each nip and pull on her nipples creating a new flood of need in her core, a core he plundered to the same driving rhythm.

This time pleasure wasn't a sudden annihilating blast, but a building pressure, promising even more destruction.

Then desperation for release overwhelmed her need to have the pleasure mushroom until it buried her, made her wail, "Too much…just *g-give* me…"

And he gave her, rode her to a crescendo that had her seizing in excruciating ecstasy, wringing every drop of his own climax with its force.

She passed out this time. She knew, because she came to with a jerk. She found Aristedes propped up on his elbow beside her on the floor—where she assumed they'd crashed during that last passionate duel—caressing her with a possessive hand on her breast and a leg between her jellified ones.

The moment she met his gaze, he gathered her and effortlessly rose with her near-swooning mass in his arms.

As he crossed to the bathroom, he nudged her ear with his lips, sending her senses haywire again with his touch, then with his words. "Now that we've taken the edge off the hunger, it's time I devoured you properly."

Selene crept around the bedroom, gathering her clothes.

The new ones he'd ordered to replace those he'd ruined, that she'd come here wearing. Two days ago.

Every time she'd thought he'd put an end to their explosive encounter, or that she should be the one to do it, he'd dragged her back into delirium. She'd ended up staying the whole weekend.

This was the only time she'd been awake while he slept.

He lay on his back, the magnificent body that had possessed and pleasured her for two long days and nights spread like a replete lion's, for the first time relaxed and unaware.

Her heartbeats tripped over each other. She wanted to rush back to him, snuggle against all that power and sensuality.

But she couldn't. This experience had been transfiguring. But now that he wasn't wringing mindless responses from her, she felt lost.

She didn't know what to do next. So she had to go.

She had to let him show her where he wanted to go from here.

Aristedes Sarantos showed her, all right.

Not personally, but in national newspapers.

Selene read the headline again.

Sarantos Leaves States After Brief Business Visit.

That was where he wanted to go from here. Away, without even a look back.

Her heart twisted.

Fool. How had she thought this could end any other way? She'd even wanted it to—why? Because of the great sex?

But if it had been only sex, how could it have been so sublime…?

Shut up. He'd just been living up to his reputation as an obsessive overachiever and conqueror.

And he'd alluded to nothing more than gorging himself on the pleasures of the moment. She'd been beyond wishful to think he'd want an encore. That their time together had been about *her* in any way.

He hadn't even uttered her name once.

She'd been a two-night, ecstatically willing outlet for whatever turmoil he'd been going through. And she should see him that way, too. It *had* been her own need for solace that had sparked her uncharacteristic abandon. He was the last man on earth she should have indulged with, making the encounter all the edgier, the riskier, wielding the power to negate her grief for as long as it had lasted. It had also been the safest outlet, letting go with the one man guaranteed to do what he'd done. Disappear after it was over without repercussions.

Now they'd go back to their old status. With one difference. She'd now inherit her father's role as his adversary.

Whatever madness had passed between them was over.

As if it had never happened.

TWO

Eighteen months later...

Déjà vu tightened its grip on Aris's senses.

Standing in front of the Louvardis mansion brought it all back. That fateful day a year and a half ago.

He couldn't believe it had been that long. Or only that long. It felt as if it were yesterday, and yet in another life.

Not that it *had* been a day, but rather a week of blows, ending in those mind-boggling two days and nights with Selene Louvardis.

His body tightened and his breath shortened, the unfailing effect the memory of that weekend had on him. Each time the slightest tendril of recollection strummed his senses, he relived the fever that had possessed him, ending in a surreal sense of fulfillment and peace, and almost total amnesia. He'd woken up remembering nothing about himself or his life, only the tempestuous, delirious time with her.

That was, until he'd realized she'd gone. The same numbness that had assailed him at that discovery spread through him again now.

It had simulated bewilderment, loss, even anger. But he'd at last decided what it was. Relief.

She'd saved him the trouble of finding a resolution to their interlude of temporary insanity. Their plunge into abandoned intimacies had been unforeseen and uncharacteristic, not to mention fraught with consequences. But they'd rushed into it like one would into danger to escape unmanageable pain.

But she'd clearly thought it better to have no morning-after, to have a clean break, resume their leashed hostilities and forget the two days they'd been all-out lovers.

He'd grappled with the need to contest that decision for hours. He'd ended up deciding it was for the best.

Respecting that unspoken treaty of avoidance had kept him away from the States since. He'd been loath to end up face-to-face with her, had feared he'd end up doing something unpredictable again.

But just as it was she who'd kept him away, now it was she—and her brothers—who'd brought him back.

He was about to crash another Louvardis function. This time, a party instead of a funeral.

His negotiators, emissaries and go-betweens had failed to resolve this current situation, the most potentially catastrophic of their business interactions. The Louvardises were no longer trying to wring him dry in negotiations. They were trying to take an ax to his throne in the shipping world. They'd left him no doubt that they would go kamikaze if it meant taking him down with them.

So he was here as a last measure. To find out just what

had instigated this extreme stance. He owed it to their father—and to Selene—to give them a chance to reach a compromise, to back off, before he employed his heaviest artillery and gunned them down.

The emotional ferocity, the lack of a logical core at this last attack had made him wonder if it was Selene's doing. But he'd dismissed that wishful thought. She wasn't a woman scorned. She was the one who'd walked out.

Whatever it was, it had to end now. One way or another.

He moved at last, passing through the gates. Good thing the man who asked for his invitation recognized him and decided to not make an issue of it. He wasn't sure how he'd have dealt with anyone coming between him and his objective, which he had to achieve with as much economy of time and hassle as possible before getting the hell out of there. This time he fully intended never to return.

He strode to the mansion's open massive oak double doors, feeling bombarded by the curiosity of those who were wandering out, cocktails in hand, to enjoy the beauty of the immaculate grounds. His ire rose with every intrusive glance. He was in worse condition than he'd thought if the violation of privacy he'd long grown an impervious shield against could rile him, and this much.

He'd better find one of the Louvardis clan, and quickly—

"I can kick you out this time, Sarantos."

Nikolas Louvardis. The one now steering the Louvardis ship, so to speak. Probably the one responsible for the current escalation in hostilities. Good. He always dealt with problems at the source.

He turned to the man the media called the "other" Greek god in the shipping business.

"Louvardis." Aris met Nikolas's brilliant blue glare

head-on, not even thinking of extending a hand he knew wouldn't be taken. Not now. But he would end this confrontation by forcing Nikolas Louvardis to put his hand in his. "It's nice to see you, too."

Nikolas's eyes filled with feral challenge. "Turn around and walk out under your own power, Sarantos. If you don't, I'm sure plenty of the attendees will capture what will happen on video and sell it to the highest bidders."

Aris huffed a mirthless chuckle. "I wouldn't mind a bit of propaganda, Louvardis. But I hear you're a piano player. Surely you won't risk your precious hands."

"Only for your jaw, Sarantos." Nikolas raised him a taunting smile. "But then again, maybe not. Your being here speaks volumes. It's actually priceless. You're scared."

Aris gave him a serene look. "Go ahead. Revel in spelling out this fascinating theory."

"Who am I to disappoint the great Aristedes Sarantos?" Nikolas bared his teeth in a smile Aris was sure would have had lesser men cringing. "So here it is. You're at the level where you have to become *the* biggest shipping mogul around, not one of a handful of kingpins, or you risk losing everything to mergers or worse. Only one thing is standing in the way of realizing your goal. Louvardis Enterprises."

"You're not the only technological-outfitting empire around, Louvardis."

"But we're the best," Nikolas countered. "With a capital *B*. If we weren't, if you had an alternative, you wouldn't be here."

"This is a two-way street," Aris said. "Now more than ever, it's vital to team up with only the best. You may be the best ship-and-port outfitters, but I'm the best ship-and-port builder."

Nikolas shrugged. "We're looking to give someone else

the chance to take that position. Want to bet whomever we choose will soon become the best?"

"Still a two-way street, Louvardis. Whomever I back, I can also make the best." Aris suddenly let the seriousness of this situation reflect in his expression. "But I'd rather not look for new collaborators. I didn't get where I am by fixing what isn't broken. Any reason *you're* trying to break it? Even your father, who cited 'irreconcilable differences' in business practices and moral standings as his reason for fighting me every step of the way, never went so far as to make it a stipulation that I be out of the picture before he agreed to sign a contract. We always managed to reach agreements that satisfied both sides. So what brought on your sudden Samson tactics?"

Nikolas scowled. "My father always fought to oust you from every major contract that involved us both. That he ended up buckling wasn't due to the power of your negotiations, but when your terrorist tactics scared his shareholders and board of directors into screaming for him to do it. And that's something we intend to rectify. You're done twisting Louvardis's arm, Sarantos."

Aris took a step closer, his stance echoing Nikolas's confrontation. "You talk as if Hektor never twisted mine. It was a draw, with me losing to you as much as I won. Especially since you and your...siblings started to pop up in the picture."

"Father recruited us—unwillingly and against his better judgment, I might add—when he felt he needed what he called 'a multipronged retaliation fueled by the fervor of new blood, the zeal of youth and the creativity of the newer generation.'"

Aris's eyes narrowed, his every sense prickling with Nikolas's barely leashed bitterness. So not everything had been picture-perfect in the family that had seemed so to him. Nikolas held the same futile resentment toward Hektor as Aris did for not appreciating his abilities, for being loath to make use of them.

Who would have thought he and Nikolas Louvardis had anything in common? And something that...essential, too?

Aris felt something yield inside him, the aggression Nikolas's baiting had ignited defusing.

His lips twitched. "But he did recruit you. And you did prove to be bigger headaches than even he ever was, taking the game to a whole new level and forcing me to be a far better player. But you, like him, know it's not in *your* best interest to alienate me."

"Alienate you?" Nikolas, back in top taunting form, barked a harsh laugh. "Try *break* you."

"Don't be foolish, Nikolas," Aris muttered, needing to bring this to where he'd always wanted it to be with this family, to the personal level. "You think losing one contract, no matter how big, can break me?"

Nikolas shrugged his immaculate shoulders, the very picture of nonchalance. "It would be the beginning of a slow but sure end for you."

Aris compressed his lips. The man seemed to be even more intractable than his father, and he hadn't thought that was possible. "You have my replacements in place? Does anyone have the resources, the experience and clout, not to mention the vision and flexibility to accommodate your needs, fulfill your demands and showcase your products? You'd end up in limbo without me, and we both know it."

"We'll worry about that when you're out of the picture."

"Don't fool yourself into thinking your father worked with me only because he was forced to. He knew I was the only one who could do his work justice."

"Maybe. But I have always despised the hell out of you, and I've never been an advocate of 'the devil you know.'"

"Let's get personal on our own time and dime, Nikolas. We have tens of thousands of futures and billions of dollars in stock riding on our decisions. You made your point, I got it. Now enough. You know you'll end up putting your hands in mine."

"Not as long as I have anything to say about it."

Aris jumped on that. "Your…siblings aren't on board on this?"

"You know what, Sarantos? You should be hailed as a miracle worker. You're the only thing my siblings and I agree on."

He should have known.

Aris exhaled. "If you force me, I'll fight you. You won't like it."

Nikolas's Adonis face radiated pure pleasure. "Ah, finally. The threats. That's more like it."

Aris exhaled again. "I'm not here to threaten you. I'm here to ask you not to force me to do that. You may believe I'm indiscriminate in my need to be the lone man on top, but if I were, I'd have crippled you and made an example of you. And even if destroying you also toppled me to the bottom rung, I would have clawed my way back to the top. I did that the first time, after all."

Nikolas's smile died and he held Aris's gaze. Unmoved, immovable. But Aris knew. Nikolas had been working to establish an equal importance in their dealings, something his father, no matter how much Aris had needed his collaboration, hadn't managed. Aris had just assured him of how much he valued Louvardis, implied his intention of granting them that equal standing in their future contracts. Nikolas wasn't shaking his hand yet, but he could feel the first signs of relenting, of appeasement.

Aris pressed his advantage. "Let me talk to your legal advisor on this contract. I'm sure we can come to an agreement."

Next second, Aris almost kicked himself.

He shouldn't have brought *her* up. Suddenly his imperturbable adversary became the irrational Greek brother who'd rather not have any male know his kid sister existed, no matter that she was one of Louvardis Enterprises' head legal strategists.

Nikolas all but grew scales and breathed fire. "You'll talk to me, or to the counselors I assign to deal with yours. *She's* not available."

"She's actually right here."

That voice.

That velvet melody, that siren song that had replayed in Aris's mind in its dizzying range of expressions. Prim in formality, ragged in emotion, abandoned in pleasure, frenzied in climax then drowsy in satisfaction. It now reverberated in his bones with the force of a nearby explosion.

She was here.

Aris swung around, Nikolas and the world disappearing as his awareness narrowed to a laserlike focus, seeking her.

And his hopes that his memories of her had been exaggerated disintegrated like a wisp of cloud under a tropical sun. For there she stood, far beyond what he'd been telling himself for a year and a half had been his wildly embellished recollections.

Even though she was walking toward them with the French door pouring sunlight at her back, she looked every inch the moon goddess she'd been named for. Tall and sure and commanding, serene and voluptuous and hypnotic, in a white pantsuit that hugged each of those curves he remembered with distressing clarity owning and exploiting, as if to taunt him that *he* no longer could. Her waterfall of ebony tresses undulated like pure darkness with the languid rhythm of her approach, and those moonlit-sky eyes shrouded in veil-of-night lashes poured royal-blue steadiness and indigo neutrality over him.

It was the challenge of her unaffectedness that managed what even his most dangerous enemies had not. They rattled the shackles of the beast he kept subjugated within him, inflamed him into unchecked frenzy, sent him roaring.

At that moment he knew.

He didn't still want Selene Louvardis.

He *craved* her.

It *had* been slow starvation that had been eating away at him, at his ability to rest, to relax, to replenish. He'd kept hoping he'd fatigue the hunger's choke hold on him until it released him. He'd been waiting to be cured. *That* was why he'd stayed away. Not to observe the logic of evasion, but from fear he'd get confirmation that what she'd aroused in him was unstoppable, unrepeatable. Indispensable.

And he'd gotten confirmation. With just one look.

That look was also enough to make him reach a resolution.

No matter the price, to anything or anyone, starting with himself, he would have Selene Louvardis again.

She stopped a few maddening steps away, a slight incline of her head sending the heavy waves of her hair cascading over her shoulder. The rich mass gleamed like a raven's wing against the whiteness wrapping her. His hands itched to weave through its luxury, to twist it around his hands, to secure her proud head by its anchor, to bend back that elegant neck for his passion.

And he would. He'd made up his mind. She would be his again.

For now he savored the abrasion of her disregard. It would only heighten the pleasure of her capitulation.

Ignoring his presence, his gaze, she focused on her brother.

"You have no call deciding what I'm available or unavailable for, Nikolas," she said, her voice even, her expression a flatline. "But the only agreement I'll reach here is with you. Any more 'talk' with Mr. Sarantos will be done through our legal teams."

Before Aris could rouse himself from the grip of fascination to think of an answer, Nikolas's phone rang.

Aris was barely aware of him as he answered it, his senses captive to Selene, until a fed-up growl broke through his fugue.

Nikolas passed Selene as he strode out of the room, muttering, "I have to go, Selene. Leave our gate-crasher to conclude his unwelcome visit and go back to the party. There are plenty of important or at least bearable people to mingle with."

Aris kept his eyes on Selene as Nikolas disappeared, monitoring her expression, trying to fathom her thoughts.

She was acting as a Louvardis, the professional whose family had decided to take him to war.

This had to be a facade. It wasn't possible the hunger gnawing at him wasn't in part in response to her own.

But she was turning away, taking her expression out of his scrutiny's reach.

"You're being an obedient kid sister and doing as your oldest brother told you?"

His words stopped her midturn, gained him her first direct look. Something quivered in his chest at the electric touch of her gaze, the exhilaration of capturing her attention, forcing her acknowledgment.

She huffed in ridicule. "You're *taunting* me into staying?"

He shrugged as he began to eliminate the gap she'd widened. "Whatever works."

Her lush lips twisted. "Yeah. That is your M.O."

He came to a halt one step away, barely stopped himself from yanking her against his buzzing flesh. "Give me one reason you shouldn't stay."

"I can give you an alphabetized index." He almost shivered with pleasure at the delicious sarcasm that roughened her voice, the deep blue fire that sparked in her eyes. "But one reason suffices. The first thing I advise my clients against is direct contact with an adversary."

He felt his lids growing heavy, his lips tautening with the growing stimulation. "We're not adversaries."

That gained him a borderline snort. It revved his excitement to higher gear. "Right. A week after my father's death, when you couldn't get around his standing orders, you maneuvered everyone into opting for another outfitter. No doubt as a first step toward removing us from your path once and for all."

"I didn't *want* someone else." Her eyes jerked wider at that. And he succumbed, wrapped aching fingers around the resilience of her arm. She lurched back a step, the look in her eyes zapping the current inside him to a higher voltage with the turbulence she could no longer disguise. He leaned closer. He wasn't letting her get away. Not again. "I still don't. But he—all of you—left me no choice. Leave me one now. I don't want us to be enemies."

And as she had that night she'd offered him solace, companionship, then mind-numbing passion, she did the unexpected again.

Instead of shaking him off, she stilled in his hold, then nodded as if to herself, before giving him a solemn glance.

"This needs to be settled."

She stepped away and started walking, heading out of the foyer and deeper into the mansion.

In minutes, he followed her into her father's old office.

It looked as if it had been kept as a shrine to Hektor. The older man's presence permeated the place. He could imagine Hektor striding in like a lion into its den any moment now, flaying him over some new disappointment.

Next second, his senses reconverged on Selene.

She was turning to him. "My father's will had something to do with you. Instructions about *what* to do with you."

He approached her again, delighting in the way she didn't let his encroachment intimidate her, met her defiance with his goading. "Is there an explanation for these instructions? Anything you agree with, or are you just following them blindly?"

She leaned back against her father's desk as if she needed the support, shrugged those strong, elegant shoulders. "He wanted to stop you from getting too big. He believed that if you did, it would cause worldwide damage to the shipping business. We agreed with each of his detailed reasons."

Aris again closed in on her. "You should at least state the charges against me before pronouncing the sentence. And then, even if I were the monster he painted me to be, knowing *you,* you're the expert in leashing all sorts of terrible entities, harnessing their potential damages into benefits for all."

Those magical eyes of hers grew opaque as she shook her head. "The decision has been made."

"Then let's unmake it. I give you my word, and any other guarantees you'd like, that what happened a year and a half ago didn't mean I wanted to be rid of you." Flames sprouted to life in the gaze entwined with his, as again bringing up the professional aspect of their relationship tripped the wires of their brief but explosively personal one. "You don't have to make a desperate dash for survival by fighting me to the death."

Her gaze flickered, echoing her waning resolve. Then she at last exhaled. "I will draft a new set of rules for our side of the operations. They'll be fair, but strict and nonnegotiable and will protect us against any future betrayals. If your claims are true, you'll agree to them."

He didn't hesitate for a second. "I will."

"If you do, I will recommend to my brothers that they resume dealing with you."

He felt the elation of wrestling with her spread through him, the fluency of their interaction, the give-and-take, which had been fully echoed in the bedroom.

His lips spread on the first real smile he could remember in years. "Then it's settled. And now that we've gotten business out of the way, let's move on to a more important topic. Us."

Her eyes became as dark as a moonless night, their temperature plunging to an arctic chill. "Listen, Sarantos—"

"Aris," he whispered. She'd called him nothing but Sarantos during their weekend together. While that had been arousing as hell, and he wanted her to keep calling him that at choice moments, he wanted to take this relationship to the next level. He wanted her to call him the nickname he'd always preferred, but that he'd never felt close enough to anyone to let them use. "That's the name I want to hear on your lips."

She pursed her lips in an attempt at severity, only making them more luscious and kissable than ever. "I prefer Sarantos. *And* to end this conversation."

He raised an eyebrow. "Give me one good reason to do that."

"Because I want to."

"And I want one thing. You."

That had her lost for words. When she finally answered, it was a cold drawl. "Why? You have another weekend to while away?"

The tone in which she said that, that she said it at all, confused him. It seemed as if she had a…grievance? Whatever for?

All he could do now was to negate her insinuation. "I've never whiled away an hour in my life. Our weekend together was incredible, incendiary. And I want more."

He could feel the same tightness that primed his every muscle for passion gripping her as she scoffed, "We've been perfectly fine not having *more* for the past eighteen months."

"*I* wasn't fine with it," he hissed with all the pent-up hunger he'd been trying to suppress. "I thought it was better not to, that I shouldn't, but I never stopped craving more."

Her gaze wavered, before she gave him a wry smile. "Welcome to the real world, Sarantos. As you so astutely worked out, you'd better not, *and* shouldn't, have everything you crave."

"Again, give me one good reason not to."

"Not to what? Spend another weekend together? I already said I'd pass." Her gaze shifted in a restless arc, seeking escape from his cornering one. "I don't have to give you reasons."

"But I don't want another weekend. I want all we can have together. Whenever it's convenient for both of us."

That yanked her gaze back to his with an openmouthed gape.

After a protracted moment, she cleared her throat. "You're proposing—for lack of a tasteful modern designation—an affair?"

He moved closer, until his thighs whispered against hers. "It's what we both need."

"But if I get you right, you're not proposing just any affair. You're negotiating an intermittent, purely sexual and no doubt secret liaison?"

He reached for her again, both hands clasping the arms she had propped against the desk. She went still in his loose hold, emotions fast-forwarding in her eyes with such volume and speed, they made his own tumble, tangle, made him dizzy with desire.

He stroked her arms, trying to transmit his urgency, his conviction. "It's all we can afford. To separate our arrangement from business, to keep the world, starting with your family, from tainting the intensity we share. And our careers are too demanding, with schedules that keep us on opposite sides of the globe. But I'll do whatever it takes so that mine allows me as many opportunities as possible to be with you. I should have proposed this a year and a half ago, shouldn't have let anything stop me from seeking the pleasures that our weekend proved only we can provide each other."

Selene's lashes swept downward, veiling her expression, making him seethe with the need to lure her gaze back to his. "You assume I want the same things."

"You *need* them. But you evidently believe you have to sacrifice your pleasures to serve your career and your family. It's how you rose so high so young. You're like me."

That had her gaze slamming back to his. The antagonism there perplexed him, yet maddened him with the need to tame it, and her.

"I'm *nothing* like you." Her voice was as hard as her glare. "And I don't take kindly to anyone deciding what I want then telling me what I need and how I need it."

She wanted a fight. A rough tussle. A demonstration of what he'd be willing to do to get her back.

He'd oblige her.

"You want and need *me*." Aris suddenly obliterated the gap between them, hauled her from the edge of the desk she'd been gripping harder by the second, slammed her against the body begging for her feel. "As for *how* you need me, if you need your memory revived, want fresh proof, I'll give it to you."

He reached behind her and swept the desk clean, sending everything crashing to the floor.

His violence jolted through her, the jumble of reactions gripping her face and body all his to decipher now. Alarm, outrage, consternation—and raging arousal.

"That's my father's stuff, you jerk…" she gasped.

He pushed her down until he had her plastered on her back against the cool mahogany, snapped open the button holding her jacket closed, spread her legs, pressed his hips between them and leaned over her. "Nothing there to be broken, and I will put them back in their exact arrangement…afterward. Now, for that proof…"

He gazed into eyes that were now like dark, stormy oceans as his hand slid down her thigh, brought it up to hook over his hip, the other diving into the silk curtain splayed around her head.

"Tell me this…" He bunched her hair around his aching fingers, wrung a moan from those full, rose-petal lips. "And this…" He lowered his head, buried his face in her breasts, inhaled the scent that had been haunting him, then opened stinging lips over one nipple after the other, nipping through her blouse and bra. He slid up to catch the gasps she rewarded him with, his tongue thrusting inside her, devouring her confession of pleasure. When her hips started undulating beneath him, he straightened, growled,

"And *this*..." He thrust his agonizing hardness against the inferno at the junction of her thighs, wringing more and more urgency from her. "Tell me *all* this wasn't what you saw, what you burned for each time you closed your eyes, awake or asleep."

She looked up at him, feverish arousal, steely defiance and something akin to...disappointment?...warring on her face.

With obvious effort, she pushed herself up on the arms she'd thrown over her head at his onslaught. Her thighs hugged his hips tighter, making his arousal jerk harder against her core.

Before he could push her back and take her then and there, she rasped, "So I have a healthy sexual appetite and you're every woman's fantasy sex partner. Too obvious to need proof."

He held her eyes for another long moment. Then, with the last iota of restraint he had, he stepped away from their intimate tangle. "I'm *your* fantasy sex partner. And you don't go around randomly satisfying your healthy sexual appetite. I bet another man would have gotten his eyes clawed out by now."

She straightened her clothes with unsteady hands. "I was thinking of the ensuing legal catastrophes that giving in to the temptation would have involved in your case."

"The only temptation you resisted was tearing my clothes off my back and clawing my flesh as you begged me to take you."

She lowered her gaze as she circumvented him on legs he knew were trembling with need. "Maybe. And maybe if you'd made this proposition after that weekend, I would have taken you up on it. It's too late now. I have someone in my life."

He almost doubled over as if from a one-two combo to the groin and gut.

He stood there as she walked to the door, vibrating like a building in the aftershocks of an earthquake.

The moment she put her hand on the doorknob, he growled, "Break it off."

She turned to him with a disbelieving glare.

He pressed on. "If you can kiss me back, want to slide under my skin, consume me whole, like you just did, it won't do him any favors if you're with him for all good cerebral reasons while you're starving for me. It will end up hurting and humiliating him."

She gave him a pitying glance. "You think you have everything in this world figured out, don't you?"

"No, but I have finally figured out what we share. If you can tell me that being with me wasn't the most intense pleasure of your life, that this other person provides you with a fraction of what you shared with me…you'll be lying. Wanting like this, compatibility like this, happens once in a lifetime, if we're phenomenally lucky. As we were, to have that weekend out of time to find each other."

She shook her head, started to turn again.

He was across the room, catching her in a second. "Say yes to me, like you did that weekend, and let's take what we need together. Break up with this…other man. I'll wait."

This time she yanked her arm away as if his touch burned her. "No. And that's a final no. We had our fling, and there's no good enough reason in *my* book to resurrect it for occasional indulgences, even of the mind-blowing variety." She opened the door, tossed him one last look over her shoulder. "You know the way by now, Sarantos. See yourself out."

* * *

Aris saw himself out. But not before he gathered the information he needed to plan her capitulation campaign.

He was damned if he'd take no for an answer. And he wouldn't wait for her to come to her senses, either. She wasn't engaged or married. So his plan was clear. He would find out who the other man was and break them up.

He'd learned that she no longer lived in the mansion, so he'd waited in his car until she left.

He tailed her to an exclusive country club, followed her inside.

He watched her stop by a woman with a baby. She greeted the woman and bent to kiss the baby before rushing away.

He rushed, too, afraid to miss her probable meeting with the man he already considered his rival. He approached the woman and the baby she'd greeted, sparing both a distracted glance.

Something he couldn't define made him take a second glance. Then a third. Then the world came to a crashing halt.

Something detonated inside his chest, threatened to expel whatever he had inside him that passed for a soul.

That baby…

That *baby*.

He was…*his*.

Three

Conviction sank through Aris like a string of depth mines.

Observations accumulated at an intolerable rate, burying him under an avalanche of details, everything that comprised this fresh, robust life.

The deep blue velvet jumpsuit that encased the baby's sturdy body. The pattern of each mahogany curl adorning his perfectly formed head. The slant of eyebrows and the press of lips that painted his face in unwavering determination as he commanded his toys' submission. The same expression he'd seen on another face, in an almost forty-year-old photo. Then came the incontrovertible sense that trumped all. That kindred tug. That blood jolt.

It was impossible, incomprehensible. It was also irrefutable. It filled every recess of his being with the first pure certainty of his life.

This was his son.

Then the baby noticed him.

The baby captured him in the bull's-eye of silver pools of endless, elemental curiosity. Slowly, answering recognition formed in their gleaming depths, beginning to radiate, then hurtle at Aris like heat-seeking missiles, skewering him through the heart and gut.

Before a reaction could form inside him, it dawned. And almost incinerated him with its advance.

A smile.

A six-toothed blow of unadulterated glee and eagerness.

Aris struggled to fill lungs that felt as if they had collapsed. Before he managed a breath, the baby moved, expelling every remaining wisp of air inside his chest, leaving it a cage tightening around an igniting coal.

He watched, mute, motionless, as that package of energy and purpose and zeal incarnate crawled in his direction as if in a fast-forwarded video. He stood there, for the first time in over twenty-five years unable to think, powerless to act, waiting for another entity's whim to decide his fate.

He looked down in total helplessness as the baby reached him, caught him in a lunging hug. Then, with the same determination with which he'd conquered his toys, the baby tried to climb his legs.

Aris felt...felt...

There were no words for what razed through him.

He stared down at the baby who was using him as a prop. The baby looked up at him and riddled his vision with the brightness of his excitement, fanning the heat inside his chest to combusting...

"Alex, come here, sweetie."

The feminine tones lashed through Aris, splitting the shell of upheaval clamping him in two. He lurched, his gaze sightlessly following the direction of the alien voice.

The woman with the baby. Dark haired and eyed, evidently Greek, a few years older than him. Neatly dressed and carefully coiffed. She wasn't looking at him but at the baby, distress on her face.

"Oh, I'm sorry, sir," she gasped. "I'll get you a wet towel to wipe this off!"

Aris stared blankly into eyes the woman now raised to his in embarrassment, watched her rush to her table, then back with the promised towel. He followed her gaze down to where the baby still clamped his legs, found him busy chewing on his pants, having already caused a sizable drool patch.

The woman swooped down on the baby, extricated him gently from around Aris's legs, to the baby's explosively vocal protest.

Aris stood rooted as the woman thrust the towel at him as she tried to get a firm hold on the now twisting, shrieking baby.

"I'm so sorry, sir," she spluttered. "I hope the stain comes out, and if not, I'm sure Ms. Louvardis will be only too happy to compensate you."

Aris numbly took the towel, stared at the woman, aware of only his mushrooming realizations.

She must work for Selene. No doubt as the baby's nanny.

Selene's baby.

Selene's baby…and his.

"I don't know what came over him," the woman went on. "Alex is usually very reticent with strangers."

Aris barely heard her, everything inside him focusing on the baby squirming in her arms. Alex was reaching his arms out to him, his silver eyes drowned in fat, trembling tears, his chubby cleft chin quivering as if he was imploring Aris to save him from a monster about to devour him.

Without volition, Aris felt his own arms rising. The woman started to loosen hers, the baby pitched toward him...

"Eleni!"

They all jerked at the harshness of the admonishment.

The woman lurched around, swinging the baby out of Aris's reach. The baby started to whimper at the rude interruption of his purpose before he suddenly gave a squee of delight. Aris raised bemused eyes, searching out the instigator of all the reactions.

Selene. She was coming back.

Aris watched her strides pick up momentum until she was streaking toward them. A lithe leopardess wreathed in deceptive white, her hair like a piece of the deepening night she was cleaving through, flying around her like angry black flames as she charged to save her cub.

"Eleni," Selene muttered as she slowed down, steps away. "Take Alex back to the cabin. Gather everything. We're leaving at once."

The woman looked stricken at Selene's sharpness, which she likely had never been subjected to. A look of guilt gripped her face as she nodded and rushed with the once again bawling baby to what Aris realized for the first time were day-use cabins surrounding a children's playground.

Then both baby and woman disappeared from his awareness, as everything converged on Selene. Selene, who was glaring up at him as if she'd like to pounce on him and rip out his neck like the leopardess his bemused fancy had just painted her as.

"What are you *doing* here?" Her eyes spewed blue fire that scorched through his numbness. "How *dare* you follow me."

He shook his head. Not to negate her accusation. To jog the shards of his shattered reason back into place.

But she wanted no answer. It had been a rhetorical question. She made that clear as, in frozen fascination, he watched her hair swirl around her in a wide arc as she swung around and started to walk away.

One step. The realizations flooding through him regressed into questions. Two steps. Questions congealed into confusion. Three. Confusion stampeded into chaos. Four. Chaos crashed into his foundations, tore at the tentacles gripping them in paralysis. Five. Paralysis disintegrated, expelled him from its grasp.

He lunged after her before she'd taken the sixth step fueled by the intention to leave him behind. He latched on to her arm.

She rounded on him, expression mirroring the same upheaval roiling inside him. "I told you to leave me alone! I told you—"

"You *didn't* tell me." Her eyes jerked wider at his ragged groan, fury draining to be replaced by wariness. And the shock and disbelief bled out of him. "You didn't tell me you had *my son*."

The truth blared on her face, blazed in her eyes. He could feel the knowledge of irrevocable exposure jolting through her, see her wrestling with a hundred reactions in succession, from shock to dismay to fear to resignation to resentment and back to fury in the space it took for his heart to punch his ribs a dozen times.

But Selene Louvardis wasn't the effective attorney she was for nothing. She could weather any shock and deal with any situation on the fly.

She straightened, presented him with her court face, collected, inscrutable, table-turning. "Why should I have told you? What does it have to do with you?"

"*You* made sure it had nothing to do with me."

His voice sounded alien in his ears, the rumble of a bewildered beast.

A tremor shook her lips before she contained it, pressed her lips into firm defiance. She wasn't as in control as she'd like him to think.

Next second he thought he might have imagined it as she shrugged, her expression implacable again, her gaze dripping icy nonchalance. "Listen, Sarantos, if you're worrying this might have repercussions for you, don't. We had consolation sex, *after* I assured you it was safe. It wasn't. I didn't factor in the hormonal mess losing my father would cause. You didn't think to check just to make sure, and I wasn't about to check with you to make sure it was okay with you if I had Alex. I'm sure if you'd known, you wouldn't have wanted him. I'm the one who did, who decided to have him. So, he's mine, and mine alone. End of story."

At that moment the nanny appeared in the distance, rushing back with a still-fussing Alex in a stroller.

Selene looked at Sarantos with the impatience of someone dying to conclude a most unpleasant topic, to guarantee no follow-up hassles. "I'm sorry you saw Alex and sorrier you recognized him as yours on sight. But really, nothing has changed. I always thought I'd end up having a baby on my own, anyway, from a sperm donor. It worked out differently, but don't think of yourself as more than that. You can go back to your life as if you didn't see this. You can also strike me off your list of available woman. Wanting me for that affair was incidental to your trip anyway, an impulse I'm sure my resistance amplified. You came to address contract terms and that has been concluded. My agreement to take you up on your business offer stands."

She turned around, making him feel she'd already left

him far behind in her mind. "Goodbye, Sarantos. I really hope our personal paths won't cross again."

This time, Aris couldn't move a muscle to stop her.

He watched her take the stroller from the nanny, steer her tiny procession out of his sight in a barely subdued hurry.

He stood there, riddled in the barrage of harsh truths she'd just bombarded him with.

She was right.

In every word she'd said.

If she'd "checked" with him, he would have said a baby was literally the last thing he wanted. Until he'd followed her here and seen Alex, the very idea of having a child had filled him with terror.

But he *had* seen Alex.

And he'd seen *her* again.

How would anything he'd ever believed about himself apply anymore?

Selene held on until she'd put Alex to bed, sent Eleni away after apologizing to her for barking at her for Aristedes's intrusion. Then she let chaos consume her.

She collapsed on her bed fully clothed, a mass of tremors.

Aristedes hadn't only found out Alex existed, he'd realized he was his.

She still couldn't believe he had from just a look.

Alex didn't resemble him *that* much, did he? If he did, why had no one else noticed? Her brothers were in the dark about the identity of Alex's father, and not for lack of guessing. They'd tried everything, from cajoling to tantrums to detective work. They'd resorted to making a list of every man she'd ever crossed paths with, then going through systematic eliminations. Aristedes was probably the only man it hadn't crossed their minds to consider.

So was it because Alex's looks could be attributed to them, since they shared physical characteristics with Aristedes? Or was it their hatred of him, their belief that she wouldn't be so stupid as to sleep with the enemy that made them unable to acknowledge the similarities? Alex did have Aristedes's hair and eyes and chin and dimple….

Her heart twisted in her chest. Seeing the two of them together tonight had been…devastating.

Since she'd discovered her pregnancy, she'd been unable to stop herself from wondering what it would have been like if things had been…different with Aristedes.

But things were what they were. And there was no changing them. As she'd known for twelve years now.

She'd always told herself her severe crush on him was a dead end because of her family's hatred of him. But she'd faced the truth of late—that the unfeasibility had been on account of his never expressing any interest in her. When he'd seemed so…prolific in his—cruelly fleeting and impersonal—interest in any unattached female who had thrown herself at his feet. That was why she'd always called herself every kind of fool for being besotted with him, not because he'd been the worst man possible to have a crush on.

Then that fateful day had come when he'd suddenly taken an interest in her, shown her that her fantasies of him had been lukewarm and pathetic. Her condition had gone from severe to distressing after those two transfiguring days in his bed.

But she hadn't been able to face waking up with him as real life reasserted itself, to await in person his verdict of how they would carry on from there.

Underneath the assured businesswoman she presented to the world was an only-and-youngest daughter of a patriarchal family. With her mother dying when she was only two, all the males in her life had thought they were compensating her by being overprotective. They'd ended up being restrictive and patronizing, even if unintentionally. She'd grown up fighting for every inch of independence she'd gained, every iota of self-confidence she'd developed.

When it came to men, after her one attempt at commitment, to escape the futility of her infatuation with Aristedes, she'd always kept her interactions with them light and distant. She'd been resigned by then that no man would ever approach her solely for her own charms, but mostly for her family's wealth and clout. Complicating her situation was Aristedes's very existence. Anyone faded to nothing in any comparison with him.

So, after the uninhibited intimacies they'd drowned in together, she'd walked away, her old self-consciousness taking hold. She'd needed him to reassure her, this man in a class of his own, that he could want her for more than a two-night stand.

But he hadn't even spared her a phone call.

Still, after her initial humiliation, she'd made excuses for him. Even after he'd eliminated Louvardis Enterprises from the contended contract only a week after her father's death, she'd been stupid enough to think that had nothing to do with *them,* that he'd had to do what was in his business's best interests. She'd kept telling herself that she couldn't have imagined the power of what they'd shared, that he'd been with her every step of the way, that he'd want to take up where they'd left off.

She'd burned for any contact from him for months before she'd been forced to face it. He was exactly what everyone said he was. An unfeeling, power-addicted, moneymaking machine. And what she'd thought so powerful had been another forgettable sexual encounter to him and she another interchangeable lay.

She'd also been unable to blame him for taking what she'd insisted on offering. There hadn't been the slightest implication of anything more, and she'd been stupid for having illusions, especially when she'd always known the truth.

She'd grown up knowing what fast and hard players were, from her brothers' example. She knew there was a subspecies of men who were all for intense but ephemeral flings, but who considered any kind of real intimacy a terminal disease. And Aristedes was worse than all of them combined. Their fling hadn't been ephemeral. It had been dizzying, devastating. And it had ended. End of story.

At least, it had been for him. For her, the story had just begun and would never end.

After coming to grips with the emotional upheaval of discovering her pregnancy, she'd told her brothers. After being stunned that their ultraresponsible, cerebral Selene was accidentally pregnant, they reverted to typical Greek male mode, demanded to know who the father was. She'd told them it was none of their business, just like it wasn't the father's. The baby was hers. And she was keeping him. Period.

And she'd had Alex. Even with all the hardships being a single parent entailed, he was the best thing that had ever happened to her. There *had* been times when she'd been worn-out enough to wish that she could have a partner in this, that Alex could have a father—Aristedes—not just his uncles for father figures. But each time reality had reasserted itself as soon as the weakness wiled those impossible wishes into her exhausted psyche. And after the first trying months passed, forging her into someone capable of weathering the daily trials of motherhood, she'd gotten more certain by the day that Aristedes would never impinge on their lives. He was gone, and he'd stay gone.

Then she'd walked in the Louvardis mansion foyer hours ago, and there he was.

Her heart lurched again at the memory of her first sight of him after all this time.

Even with his back to her, even just hearing his voice locked in a testosterone-driven verbal brawl with Nikolas, he'd brought the tempest of longings and insecurities crashing back through her, scattering her stability and self-assurance.

Only the need to drive him away—before his presence caused a ripple effect that would mess up her orderly existence—had made her announce herself and attempt to speed up his departure.

It had turned out to be the worst thing she could have done.

Was it any wonder? She seemed unable to make one decision, take one action, have one thought that didn't end in catastrophe where Aristedes Sarantos was concerned.

Instead of walking away, she'd confronted him. Instead of playing along, she'd defied him. Instead of clawing his eyes out, she'd almost succumbed to the ecstasy only he wielded.

And her challenge had reignited his interest. He'd even offered to make her his Stateside mistress. Another flavor in the assortment of eager bodies he no doubt had in every port.

And the worst part? She'd been outraged, disappointed, insulted. But she'd also been tempted.

She could no longer even attempt to deny it.

She still wanted him. Still craved him.

Well, so what if she did. She was only a woman. And there was no way any female with a pulse wouldn't want that hunk of premium virility.

Her predictability made no difference. Just as she didn't

devour every piece of chocolate fudge cake that cast its spell on her, she wouldn't have *him*. She wouldn't come near him, or let him come near her. Or Alex.

Not that he'd want to do either now.

He'd probably grope for his walking papers, her absolution, and disappear into the sunset, this time never to return.

Selene had a newly minted conviction.

Whoever had dreamed up Greek gods had evidently had no idea someone like Aristedes Sarantos would one day exist and far surpass their imaginings.

And contrary to her expectations, he hadn't disappeared.

Worse. He'd returned.

She watched Dina flutter as she led him in, almost flooding Selene's spacious office in drool.

Selene barely held back from rolling her eyes when she had to gesture for her smart, savvy and searingly sarcastic PA to stop panting over Aristedes and leave them alone.

Not that she was in any better condition herself. She'd just had much more practice in hiding the chaos this man caused inside her. Though *chaos* was too harmless and peaceful a word to describe what his presence here was kicking up.

The one thing that helped keep it unmanifested was rationalizing said presence. He had business details to negotiate.

She didn't rise from her desk. She doubted her legs would support her. And before he came closer, drew her deeper into his field of influence, she had to abort his mission.

"You should have called before coming," she said. "I'll text you when I draft the new terms. It'll be at least a week."

That failed to stop him. He didn't even stop when he reached her desk. He came around it. Then he was towering over her, the raw power and masculinity barely harnessed within the deceptively civilized trapping of immaculate darkest gray silk pants searing her flesh through her own flimsy protective layer.

She couldn't even swing away, trapped as she was in that heavy-lidded and -lashed gaze capable of slicing through steel.

Heat surged from that place inside her that she kept under tight containment, a furious fountain of excitement, of life, which she'd been keeping on an even trickle of steadiness and coping.

He made it worse, drawled, "I'm not here to talk business."

That something in the center of her being crackled, snapped.

She didn't resist this time. She should just give in. Just one more time. Capitulate, negate her challenge, break his thrall.

She'd let them have this release, this closure, here, now.

The words of her one-shot surrender trembled on her lips.

He quelled them. With his next words.

"I'm here to offer a new proposition. Marry me."

Four

Marry me.

Aris had believed he'd live and die without ever uttering those two words.

But even if his wildest fantasies could have painted this impossible scenario, they wouldn't have expanded to imagining the reaction the offer would elicit.

After gaping at him for minutes on end, stupefaction a frozen mask on her face, Selene now seemed to be choking.

But she wasn't choking.

Selene was laughing. So hard she could barely breathe.

Every crystalline peal fell on him like a resounding slap.

Not that he could even blame her.

If anyone had asked him yesterday what would be the most ridiculous thing he could think of, considering marriage as even a theoretical option for him, let alone proposing in practice, would have been at the top of his list.

It evidently ranked way up there on the echelons of the absurd to her, too.

He exhaled in resignation, braced his legs apart, shoved his hands deep in his pants' pockets and brooded down on a sight he'd never thought to see. Selene Louvardis, helpless in the grip of a fit of laughter.

He wondered how he would have felt if this was fueled by delighted mirth, not stunned ridicule.

He found his teeth gritting tighter as he watched her every nuance and waited for her amusement to die down. At last, she reached across her desk for a tissue to wipe away tears, shaking her head as if she still couldn't credit that she'd heard him say what he'd said.

Then she finally looked up at him, disbelieving mockery staining her gaze and twisting one corner of that edible mouth.

He sighed. "I bet you wouldn't have laughed that hard if I'd proposed that you adopt me."

Another chuckle burst out of her. "I would have actually found that a more feasible proposition." She shook her head again. "That's the one thing I have to give you, Sarantos. You're so totally, predictably unpredictable, you thwart all those who analyze you to chart what you'll do next. Conglomerates have bet their futures on you jumping one way then you always go and do something this…ridiculously outrageous, and leave everyone staring in your wake in incomprehension. Marry you, huh? Phew. Wow. I didn't see *that* one coming." Suddenly the shrewdness in her eyes rose to overshadow everything else. "I bet even *you* are wondering what the hell you think you're doing."

He gazed down into those mocking eyes. They reminded him of the pristine moonlit skies of his childhood where the stars had twinkled secret communications of consolation and wisdom to him. He felt their gaze penetrate down to his bones, seeing right through his apparent certainty to his turmoil.

He might act as if he'd worked out all the ramifications of this proposal, knew what he was asking. But he hadn't. He didn't.

Did anyone, who ever proposed something so irreversibly life-changing?

He *had* been dreading her reaction. And he didn't know which of the possibilities he'd dreaded more. Shock, suspicion, anger, hesitation, elation, coyness, rejection, acceptance, a combination of some or a sequence of all. Each one opened a gateway to a hellish realm he would have done anything to step clear of.

But he shouldn't have worried. She'd defied them all.

He shook his head, too, holding that gaze that asked for no quarter and gave none. "*You* should talk about unpredictability."

"You mean you didn't see this…fit coming in answer to your imperative demand? If you didn't, I've either gravely underestimated your arrogance, or you're losing your infallible insight and preternatural powers of prediction."

Now that he thought about it, with his growing knowledge of her, outright ridicule—the one reaction he'd left out of the possibilities—should have been the only one he expected. And he should be relieved.

He wasn't.

He had no idea why he wasn't. He no longer knew anything. Not how he felt, or how to deal with the discoveries that had decimated his every meticulously constructed concept of himself, uprooted every ironed-out-to-the-last-detail strategy of his life.

So here he was, doing what he hadn't done since he

was twelve. Jumping without a plan, let alone a backup. Improvising. Because for the first time, he could see no other viable option.

He finally exhaled. "It's probably a mixture of both."

Her gaze wavered. She hadn't thought he'd admit to either charge, let alone both, and that willingly?

Before he could be sure of his analysis, steely challenge flooded back into her expression. "So, I'll spell out the question you're asking yourself. What the hell do you think you're doing, Sarantos?"

His lips twitched at the baiting in her gaze, even as something there compressed his chest over what felt like thorns. A white-hot kernel of affront? Of fury? Of…hurt?

No. He'd just admitted his perception was on the fritz. It might have always been where she was concerned. He should no longer try to fathom her or himself. He should let this play out, take him where it would. He'd help it along with the one thing that he had to contribute now. Straightforwardness.

He emptied his gaze of all but seriousness. "I'm doing what I have to do. I'm asking you to marry me."

Flames of that elusive expression flared, raged higher. His chest began to burn. Then she seemed to douse them with an act of pure will, smirked. "There he goes again. Okay, let me get this straight, Sarantos. You're going for your most unpredictable by being predictable for once? You're offering to 'marry me' because I 'had your son,' just like any dutiful male would? How quaint."

This was serious. This confrontation was not going according to any unformed fears he might have come here harboring. But he couldn't help it.

Her belittling barbs penetrated right to his humor centers, tripped their wires.

His lips spread. "You make it sound as if I'm a different species."

Something heavy and hot entered her gaze, made the tightness travel lower in his body. It was uncanny, unprecedented, how she took control of his body with a look. That particular look now grew antagonistic.

"You know you *are* a different species, Sarantos," she muttered. "Trying on the conformities of a member of the common herd doesn't suit you."

He exhaled. "Not conforming was a luxury I availed myself of for the past twenty-five years. Under the circumstances, I can no longer afford it."

Her gaze hardened with each word out of his mouth. "Do you even hear yourself? Just yesterday you were offering the ultimate form of disconnection in human liaisons. Then you discover Alex and switch to proposing the ultimate form of entanglement, the stuck-till-death kind of situation, or the type of mistake with escalating consequences."

His gaze stilled. Did that mean she had as dismal a view of marriage as he'd always held?

Neither his beliefs nor hers were the issue here. They both had another—*Alex*—to consider now.

He nodded. "I am aware of the discrepancy. But the givens of the situation have changed diametrically since."

She exhaled her impatience. "It seems I have to repeat what I said last night, in a clearer way. You have nothing to do with Alex or me. There's no duty or right thing to do involved here."

"If I didn't believe there's all of that and more involved, I wouldn't be here today."

She seemed at a loss for words. Then she rasped, "I'll make it clearer still. An offer of marriage for a baby's sake means you're applying for the positions of husband and father. In which parallel universe are you husband and father material, Sarantos?"

Silence seemed to explode in the wake of her bluntness. An evaluation, an exposure he wasn't about to contest.

Not that she was giving him the chance to waste her time with protests when she'd long made up her mind about him. "You're not any known human relationship material, either. Even with your siblings, you have the most perfect example of nonrelationships."

He wasn't about to contest that truth, either.

He let his no-contest count as an admission, went on to make his point, the only one to be made here. "I may well be the last man on earth to qualify for either role, but that doesn't change the facts. You had my child. A child I owe my name and support. I owe you that, too."

She hooted in pure denigration. "Whoa. At least no one can accuse you of spouting sentimental embellishments. Tell you what. The 'child' and I will take a rain check on whatever you believe you owe us. In this life. Let's take this up again in another. We're both fine for this one, thank you."

"Being 'fine' isn't a reason not to accept my support and protection, to benefit from my status and wealth."

"I say it's the perfect reason not to. I don't need support and protection, and I have status and wealth, and so will Alex. What else do you have to offer us?"

Everything stilled inside him at the lethal conciseness of her question. She always managed to take truth to its most abrading foundations.

And he had to offer her the same level of brutal frankness.

"I have no idea," he said. "Probably nothing."

Another silence crackled in the wake of his admission. Then her lips made a luscious twist of cynical certainty.

"There you go. And thank you for not pulling punches. It saves us from wading through false sentiments and promises, which have no place between us."

The oppressive tightness in his center, what always signaled things spiraling out of control, heightened.

He shook it off, countered, "I do think so, too, if for an opposite reason. It's exaggerated expectations that destroy any endeavor, personal or professional. I am offering you the absolute truth, so you'll know for certain what I'm offering."

"But *you* are not sure what you're offering," she shot back.

"Besides everything you claim not to need, no, I'm not sure," he said. "But honesty trumps false security every time."

"And, like your offer, it's still deficient and unnecessary. And the reason behind both your honesty and your offer is even worse."

He'd thought she'd hit him with all she had, that he could now begin to negotiate. Seemed she was far from done.

He cocked one eyebrow at her, genuinely interested, even impatient, to find out what else she would hit him with. "So what terrible motive have you come up with for me?"

"It seems that even you haven't escaped the social conditioning that stipulates that men must take responsibility for their progeny or forfeit their right to manhood and its pride and privileges." She swung her chair back to her desk, swept him a sidelong glance that had the heat percolating beneath his ribs spreading to his head before flooding the rest of his body. "So I'm judging your motives are a cocktail of pride, honor and responsibility."

He stared at her. *That* was what she'd thought so bad?

He barked a guffaw of incredulity. "You say it as if those are the most reprehensible of motives."

She inclined her head, making his hands itch when the movement sent a swath of midnight silk swishing over one turquoise-clad shoulder. "They're up there with the worst kind of motives in my opinion. You don't marry someone, or become someone's father, because your unreasoning male pride is prodding you, a reluctant sense of honor is harassing you or a hated responsibility is breathing down your neck."

Just yesterday, if they'd had that same conversation, he would have said the same things, in as harsh or harsher terms. He'd always believed if something was wrong, it was wrong no matter the circumstances. But maybe he'd been wrong.

He exhaled his deepening uncertainties. "Maybe a lot of men don't start out in a marriage having those motives, but most stay because of that glue of pride and honor and responsibility."

She took her gaze away completely now, busied herself with arranging some papers on her desk. "Maybe. And maybe other women have to accept that, because alternatives are far worse. That is not true in my case. Appeasing your sense of duty and male pride isn't good enough for me, or for Alex. Your name, money and status are all you're offering because they are all you have *to* offer. And since they don't feature as reasons for me to marry, they don't count for me. As for you, in case you're trying to contain a situation you fear will one day take a far bigger bite out of you than the price you're willing to forfeit to deal with said situation in its…infancy, so to speak, I again assure you…" She suddenly looked up, slammed him with a solemn stare. "Neither I nor Alex will ever need a thing from you. I can guarantee you that in a binding contract."

She was making this hurdle course harder with every look, every word. He hadn't come prepared to engage her in a grueling character dissection. Grappling with his own doubts and deficiencies had commandeered most of his resources. He'd expended the rest in making the offer at all. Now he was down to his reserves, and she was depleting those fast.

Her cell phone rang. She lunged for it as if for a raft in a stormy sea.

He watched the metamorphosis of her expression as she took what was evidently an unwelcome business call. So that was how she looked when she was dispassionate, formal, as he'd thought she'd been as she'd confronted him. But seeing the real thing now made him realize she'd actually been seething with emotions. Mostly negative, granted, but they were fierce and specific to him, and he was their instigator and their target.

How had he been fool enough not to include that intensely personal factor in his negotiation?

He waited for her to end her call then closed the two steps he'd kept between them, bent and clamped both her wrists in his hands. Her gaze jerked up to his, her face an unguarded display of surprise and vulnerability as he tugged her out of her seat and against the body that clamored to feel her against it.

He held eyes that had emptied of all but instant response, savored her instinctive surrender before she snapped back into antagonist mode.

"There *is* one more thing I can offer," he groaned. "One thing you know only I can offer. This…"

He swooped down and stilled the tremor invading the fullness of her lower lip in a bite that made her cry out, arch into him, all lushness and urgency. The taste and feel and scent of her flooded his senses, eddied in his arteries, pounded through his system. She spilled gasps into his mouth, her tongue sliding against his, tangling, her teeth matching him nip for nip, until he felt himself expanding, as if he'd unfold around her, devour her whole. And he'd only intended to kiss her, make his point. He should have known he'd lose his mind at her reciprocation.

He gathered her pants-clad thighs, opened her around his hips, pinned her to the wall behind her desk with the force of his hunger. She clung to him, arms and legs, opening for his tongue, for the thrust of his arousal against her heat through their barriers.

He felt his brain overheating, his body hurtling beyond his volition. Only one thing would stop him from taking her against that wall. Her. He wouldn't stop otherwise. Which he should, before the point he'd intended to make in his favor became more proof against him.

Suddenly, as if she'd heard his feverish thoughts, she was writhing against him in a different kind of desperation, to get away.

He stilled, snatched his lips from hers, raised his head to roam unseeing eyes through the black-and-blue blankness of frustration, only to drop his forehead against hers, sharing the upheaval of aborted passion.

When he could finally make a move that didn't drive his body against hers, he unclamped her from his spastic grasp and let her down on her feet.

He still couldn't move away. It was she who did, stumbled around him on unsteady legs without meeting his eyes. His body roared anew as she brushed past him, as he realized he'd undone her blouse, had her breasts almost spilling from her bra. Before he could send everything to hell and pounce on her, drag her to the ground, give them both what they were in agony for, she put the width of her desk between them, began to speak.

For a moment he saw nothing but those lips that had just been suckling coherence right out of him, glistening and swollen from his possession. He could imagine nothing but them moving like that, all over him.

It was only when he heard her say "...I want you..." that his mind screeched its stalled wheels to process her words.

Then he realized the context of her words, and that was a far more efficient libido douser than a plunge in freezing waters.

"If you wanted to prove that I want you," she said, her breath still ragged, her face flushed, "and that you'd offer great sex in the new bargain, as I told you last night, you shouldn't have bothered. We both already know that." She picked up the dossier she'd gathered earlier, started to walk to her office door. "Now if you'll excuse me, I have a meeting."

He prowled toward her, trying to keep his approach, his stance, unthreatening as he blocked her way. "I was only bringing up benefits both of us were overlooking while we analyzed what I have to bring to the table."

She swept away the bangs his passion had spilled into her eyes, looked up at him with something that chilled him. An emptiness he'd never seen.

"So you're combining yesterday's offer and today's— no-strings sex merged with a legal union for damage control?"

He didn't know what to say when she put it that way. It *was* what he was offering, but stripped of any humanity and stated in the stark terms only a lawyer could reduce it to.

But she was waiting for him to say something. So he did. "This is far more than what most so-called couples have."

Her gaze lengthened for seconds before she nodded.

His heart lurched in his rib cage. Did she agree?

Before he could think of anything more to say,

she circumvented him wordlessly, resumed her path to the door.

Once she opened it, she turned to him. "As a business-woman, I enter only into ventures where the pros outweigh the cons. In your case, Sarantos, all the pros in the world don't counter your cons. So my answer to your proposition is no. And I demand you take this no as final and nonnegotiable."

Aris watched as the door closed behind her with muted finality, and wondered.

What the hell had he done?

"You did *what?*"

Selene winced at the sharpness of her best friend's cry of disbelief.

Worse than disbelief. Kassandra Stavros's sea-green eyes were explicit with the conviction that Selene had gone mad.

Kassandra was the only one she'd told her secret. But that wasn't why she'd told her what had happened with Aristedes. Kassandra had just happened to walk in on her at her most distraught after he'd left a couple hours ago.

Not that she'd told her everything. Just the bare bones of the two climactic confrontations they'd had since yesterday. She certainly hadn't mentioned the temporary insanity that assailed her every time Aristedes touched her....

Now she wished she had a rewind-and-erase function. She would have wiped Kassandra's memory. She would have wiped hers, of the meetings with Aristedes. Of Aristedes himself.

"You'd be nuts if you turned him *down* down." Kassandra spelled out her view of Selene's mental stability. "And since you're the most un-nuts person I know, you didn't, right?"

"*Down* down?" Selene huffed. "As opposed to down *up?*"

Not picking up on Selene's dejection, but only the derision, Kassandra made a face at her. "You know what I mean. Down for real. You're making him sweat it, right? I won't say he doesn't deserve it, 'cause he does, big-time, for walking away without a look back and staying gone that long."

"Don't forget coming back for business then tossing me an incidental proposition to be his sporadic sex stop in the States."

Now that Selene was being sarcastic, Kassandra took her words seriously, nodded in all earnestness, her dainty nose crinkling in disgust. "Sure, for that, too. That actually deserves some creative grovel-inducing punishment. The nerve of that man." Suddenly Kassandra's lips twisted as she sighed. "But what a man. You have to admit, if anyone can get away with arrogant bullshit like that, it's him."

A spark of sick electricity quivered behind Selene's breastbone.

She'd always seen that glazed look come into women's eyes at the mention of Aristedes. And even if Kassandra was just indulging in the indiscriminate drooling most women did over hunky strangers, that it bothered *her,* and so much, made her mad. *And* sure that she'd done the right thing by turning Aristedes *down* down.

She didn't do jealousy, would have hated herself and her life if she'd ended up with a man every woman lusted after. A man whom she knew could never be hers, with whom she'd suffer that soul-destroying sickness, never sure if he was lusting back, or worse.

She now found herself imagining how Aristedes would react to her childhood friend. Kassandra, the rebel who'd gone against her strict Greek family's will and become a top model and rising fashion designer, was a golden goddess. Aristedes, like all other men, would no doubt pant after the willowy grace and screaming femininity of her friend's body, the masses of incredible sun-streaked hair and those Mediterranean green eyes. But contrary to her reaction to most other men, once she knew Aristedes wasn't Selene's territory, Kassandra would pant back, and more.

Unaware of the disturbing thoughts spreading their hated tentacles through Selene's mind, and bent on concluding her train of thought, Kassandra went on excitedly, "So, how long will you make him suffer? I say at least a day for each month. And maybe another week for that last transgression."

"Kass, I'm not going to make him sweat or salivate or anything else. I turned him *down* down."

After gaping at her for a long moment, Kassandra shook her head. "A knee-jerk reaction. Understandable. But definitely not the right one." Her focus sharpened on Selene. "So marriage was never on your agenda after that so-called engagement fiasco with Steve, no matter how much your family pushed you. I think they contributed to your eternal self-sufficiency with that constant stream of eligible and terminally boring bachelors. But you're almost thirty years old, you aren't saving yourself for a man you fancy more, since you fancy the hide off that one—so much so you broke your vow of celibacy for him *and* had a son with him, for chrissake! And since he offered marriage, who better to marry?"

"Who worse," Selene muttered. "This man is my family's enemy. *My* enemy. Until proven otherwise. And even that proof is something he can—and did in the past—negate in a heartbeat if he thought he'd make a million dollars more by turning against us."

Kassandra shook her head. "That's business."

"And *personally* he cares nothing for me," she said, trying to strip her voice of any emotional charge. "Or for Alex. Whatever he's offering, he's doing it for sterile reasons with no human factor involved. One of my father's biggest objections to him was the way he treated his family. Six younger brothers and sisters he plied with checks in lieu of affection and services instead of having an actual role in their lives. Even when his youngest brother died, he didn't stay with his family to console them for a single night. And I won't let what happened to his siblings happen to Alex. It's better for him not to know his father than to have a father who'll make him feel alienated and worse than fatherless."

Kassandra chewed her lips. "Hmm, I didn't know it was that bad. But, cut the guy some slack. A man who built an empire without a formal education after the age of twelve, starting with a fishing boat at the age of fourteen, must be real busy. As I said, normal rules don't apply to him. Maybe there are things about him that would make up for what a normal man would provide."

Kassandra's efforts to make her look at the bright side spread more darkness inside her. "Not according to his siblings, there aren't." Before Kassandra could bounce back with another sales pitch on Aristedes's behalf, Selene pressed on. "There's also the catastrophe currently brewing between him and my family. He might *say* he'll do anything to stop it, but he'll probably take one look at the new terms I'll lay out and tell me to go to hell, then open fire on all of us. Plus, my brothers have been seething ever since they found out about my pregnancy. If their testosterone-driven collective finds out Alex is his, I have two predictions. Either they'll gang up on him and tear him limb from limb, or they'll gang up on him and me and force us into a shotgun wedding."

"But the guy won't need to be forced into a wedding! He already offered."

"Sure. And when I refused he must have felt so relieved, and probably righteous to boot. Now he can go back to his hard business and fast women with a clear conscience. If he has one."

Kassandra looked at her, her green eyes filled with the need to shake her, and the need to hug her, console her.

Kassandra finally let her shoulders slump. "At least give yourself some time to think about it. For me? I'd love to design your wedding dress. I'll design you a whole trousseau!"

Selene hugged her friend, loving her more for persisting in trying to talk her out of what she evidently thought a terrible mistake.

But Selene knew the biggest mistake would be to let an emotionally stunted and unavailable man like Aristedes—no matter how much she craved him, no matter that he was her son's father—into her life.

Selene woke up after a harrowing night of wrestling with tentacles trying to drag her into a bottomless abyss.

The worst part had been when she'd wanted with everything in her to succumb to their pull.

Though Alex was still asleep, evidenced by his tranquil breathing on the baby monitor at her bedside table, she rushed to his nursery. She always needed to see him first thing in the morning, but today, the need was a gnawing urgency.

On her way to Alex's room, the bell rang.

She stopped in the hallway, squinted up at the wall clock. Eight a.m. Eleni's usual arrival time.

Then Selene remembered. Today was Saturday. Eleni wasn't coming. Selene gave her weekends off since she didn't let Alex out of her sight, making up for the time she spent away from him during the workdays.

So who could it be, this early?

She rushed to the door with terrible scenarios chasing each other through her head. She snatched it open, and...

Aristedes was standing there, in the first casual outfit she'd ever seen him in, immaculate in light blue denim, overpowering in influence. He was brooding down at her, his eyes simmering like steaming ice in the dim golden lights illuminating the spacious, ultrachic corridor leading to her apartment door.

She stared up at him.

Nothing had changed, or would ever change.

Yet all she wanted was to drag him inside, devour him and tell him she'd take whatever he had to offer.

Everything she'd held at bay flooded over her. The longing she'd suppressed. The loneliness and depression she'd suffered during her pregnancy and Alex's early months. The resignation that she'd be a mother, a businesswoman, a sister, a friend, but never a *woman,* never like she'd been with him, for as long as she lived.

And she knew she had to do it. Make him an offer of herself without a safety net, just to end this alienation, just to experience that level of intimacy, that state of acute... *living* she could only attain with him...

She started, "If you're here to see if I changed my mind, I—"

He cut off her wobbling offer. "I'm here to say I changed mine. I want you to forget everything I proposed to you."

Five

Selene stared up at Aristedes and understood at last.

Why he was generally known as the devil.

Aristedes Sarantos was an insidious, maddening, heart-stealing, soul-stripping tormentor. He kept coming at those he wanted to control or conquer like said devil, persistent, tireless, endlessly persuasive one moment, overwhelmingly seductive the next. Then when he had his victims in too deep, he churned them dry of everything that made them themselves with all the mercilessness of a capricious, indifferent ocean. Everyone invariably buckled before him, their stamina depleted, their wills eroded.

Aristedes had told her that her father had died after he'd ranted at him. She hadn't been able to imagine what had driven her father to such a fit of frustration with his longtime sparring partner. Aristedes's latest terms hadn't been any more exasperating or restrictive than any he'd made in the past. She'd thought that her father's approaching death had brought on that uncharacteristic outburst, not the other way around.

But right now, she could see how wrong she could have been. How Aristedes could have chipped away at her father's endurance, until he'd snapped, at a seemingly unrelated moment.

He'd done the same to her. He'd submerged her under his spell, addicted her to ecstasies only he could provide before casting her out. He'd crossed her path again just to repeat the sadistic game.

In the past two days he'd reignited the dormant sickness inside her, watched her struggle against it, pretended to let her escape only to pursue her again, until she wanted nothing but the reprieve of plummeting into his trap. Then he told her that he wasn't even going to catch her in it, would let her fall to her fate, whatever it was….

No. She wouldn't let him destroy her like he had her father, like he had so many others. He'd damaged her enough already, but solely because she'd let him. She'd protect herself at whatever cost. She no longer possessed the luxury of risking injury. She didn't belong just to herself any longer. She must do whatever it took to keep her mind intact and her soul whole. For Alex.

She couldn't translate her resolutions into action. He still held her in his inescapable thrall. And she wondered whether he would start laughing like a devil from an old melodrama.

But he merely exhaled. "You were right to turn me down. And when you said I didn't know what the hell I was doing."

It wasn't what he said that had the steel of rage infusing her bones, the magma of outrage replacing her blood. It was that expression on his rugged face, that amalgam of earnestness and self-deprecation.

She found her voice at last, found the words that would not betray the blow he'd dealt her. "Thanks for letting me know. You didn't have to come all the way here, though. You could have just let it go. I did leave you yesterday with the understanding that this case is closed."

Before the hot needles behind her eyes dissolved into an unforgivable manifestation of stupidity and weakness, she began to close the door she found she'd been clutching with a force that was almost damaging her fingers.

The door stopped against an immovable object. His flat palm.

"I can't just accept that," he said, his voice low, leashed.

What did her tormentor mean now? Was he ending one game to start another?

She raised eyes as bruised as her self-respect to his, found them void of anything but solemnity and determination.

Before she could cry out her confusion and chagrin, he elaborated on his statement. "I never let anything go unless I'm certain it's unworkable. I now realize I made you two unworkable offers, and that's why I'm withdrawing them. But I'm here to offer something else. A workability study."

Feeling her legs wobble, she leaned against the door, thankful for its support and partial shield. "Alex and I are not a business venture you can test for feasibility."

His gaze grew darker, deeper, made her feel he was trying to delve into her mind, take control of it. "It's actually the other way around. It is I who would be tested."

She shook her head, her bewilderment growing. "Why bother? I know, and *you* know, that you're not... workable."

His spectacular eyebrows dipped lower over eyes she

felt were now emitting silver hypnosis. "You're right, again. Neither you, nor I, have any reason to believe that isn't the truth. The only truth. It might be the best thing for both you and Alex to never hear from me again, to forget I exist. But then again, maybe not. I'm asking only for the chance for both of us to find out for certain. You believe I'm…unworkable in any personal relationship. I've lived my life based on this same belief about myself. I've never had reason to question or test it. I have one now. I have two."

She stared at him, lost in the tangles of the contradictions he'd bombarded her with.

She struggled to rasp past the heart bobbing in her throat. "But you already admitted you were wrong when you rashly applied for the positions of part-time legal lover and father."

He was watching her now with an intensity that made her feel he wanted to steer her thoughts and actions. Which she wouldn't put past him—wanting to do it, or succeeding in doing it.

He finally nodded. "I agree that being a biological father to Alex doesn't mean I'm entitled, or qualified, to be his father for real, part-time or otherwise. And being your two-night lover doesn't mean I can be…any more than that. But I want to find out what I *can* be, for both of you."

She opened her mouth, closed it, before blurting out, "Why would you want to be anything at all for either of us?"

His sculpted lips twisted. "I think that is self-explanatory."

"Not to me. You don't do relationships of any sort, remember?"

"I never forget. But this isn't about the past, it's here

and now and we're both in a situation we've never been in before. I think we owe it to ourselves—and to Alex—to find out what we can, or can't, be to each other."

"How exactly would we find that out?" Her voice was almost inaudible in her own ears now.

His voice was just as soft, as hushed when he simply said, "Give me today."

She gaped at him.

After moments when neither had even breathed, he inhaled. "If I'm to be tested for…workability, I have to be put to the test in your everyday reality with Alex. If today works without major objections on both your parts, we'll take it from there."

She took two involuntary steps back, as if from the precipice of an active volcano. "I—I don't think that's a good idea. And don't ask me to give you reasons why I think it isn't."

He compensated for the steps she'd pulled back, taking him over her threshold and inside her condo.

And all she could think as she watched his intimidating perfection fill her foyer was that he was really here. She'd been resigned that she'd never see him here. In her inner world, in the sanctum she'd created for herself and Alex.

But she'd imagined it, against her better judgment, so many times, in so many scenarios.

Reality was nothing like her fantasies. More vivid, overwhelming, messing with her mind. She felt breached, exposed, invaded. And he'd just taken one step inside her condo, hadn't even touched her.

"I don't think it's too much to ask." Just the touch of his eyes, the caress of his voice shook her to her core. She started to shake her head again and he went on, "In the world out there, I'd be entitled to far more, if I were to enforce my rights."

This made her malfunctioning resistance rev from zero to one hundred. She bristled. "Are you threatening me?"

"No." His level gaze told her he meant it. And fool that she was, she believed him. "I'm just pointing out that I do have rights to Alex."

Her heart wrenched as his words snapped open an image of an abyss beneath her feet.

She struggled not to let the dread bursting inside her show, camouflaged it in defiance. "But not to me."

He blinked, slowly, an unequivocal consent. His tone was as weighed down and profound. "I'm not demanding any, to either of you. I'm asking for a…gift. A day. Give it to me, Selene."

She felt as if the building had been hit with an earthquake.

The floor beneath her feet rocked, a crash of thunder detonating, drowning all thoughts, traversing her being.

It was the first time he'd ever uttered her name.

And on his lips, it was no longer a name. It was an invocation, a spell.

Before she could succumb to either, or deal with the aftershocks of his employing the weapon he'd been reserving until drastic measures were needed, he released her from his influence.

He raised his eyes, cast his gaze above her head, his whole body tensing, reminding her of a great cat priming for an all-out run.

Then his voice dipped an octave lower. "He's awake."

She stared at him in incomprehension for a moment, before she heard it, too. Alex's usual wake-up babble.

He lowered his eyes to her, and time seemed to warp. Her senses, too, since she couldn't really be seeing this on

Aristedes's face, sensing it blasting off of him. Amazement, vulnerability, transforming his hard, unyielding beauty into a mask of pliable wonder.

As insane as it seemed to her, she thought he was experiencing the same thing she felt every time she heard her son's self-entertaining noises. Pure and instant heart-melt.

Suddenly the noises stopped. Then a wail went off, severing her nerves wholesale.

Panic exploded inside her, propelling her around, sending her streaking with all senses zooming ahead of her to the nursery. She barely heard her condo door slam shut, reverberating the sitting area's windows, or the masculine footsteps almost overlapping with hers in a staccato of urgency on her polished hardwood floors.

She burst into the nursery. It was cloaked in darkness. But she knew the unobstructed path to Alex's crib by heart, hurtled there, even as she realized his wails had died down to be replaced by noises of exertion.

"I'm here, sweetie," she gasped as the blackout curtains were drawn open, flooding the room in the cool sunlight of New York City's early April morning.

She realized it was Aristedes's doing as she anxiously surveyed Alex and came to a stop beside his crib. It seemed he'd again tried to climb out of it and failed, bringing on that explosive fit of frustration before he'd picked himself up and had been trying again when they'd burst into the nursery.

Alex blinked, adapting to the sudden light, before focusing on her and gifting her with that single-dimpled, soul-possessing smile of his. He reached out his chubby arms to her, part delighted to see her, part finding her a solution to his dilemma. She reached down to him as eagerly, her fright draining.

She picked him up, hugged his warm, resilient body to her heart, inhaled his beloved scent as she kissed his downy cheeks, cooing good-morning to him and soft chastisements about being in too much of a hurry to leave his infancy behind. He burrowed his face into her bosom like a delighted kitten, gurgling his contentment. Then he stilled, snapped up his head, his eyes rounding as he gazed over her shoulder, his flushed lips, the miniature of Aristedes's, forming an adorable O of astonishment.

She swung around, found Aristedes standing a pace away, dwarfing them, making her feel as if he could contain them both inside his great body. He was looking at Alex, a stunned expression in his eyes, the rest of his face frozen.

She heard the sharpness of his indrawn breath when Alex pitched from her arms, lunging toward him, arms wide-open in an imperative demand to be held.

Alex had never reached out to anyone like that. Not even his uncles, who'd been around since he was born—he'd let them hold him only after she'd encouraged him, hugged them and showed him they were safe and dear to her.

She'd thought the first time he'd done this with Aristedes had been a fluke. That he'd been upset with Eleni and had been seeking to escape her hold by commanding the only other adult around to remove him from her grasp.

But there was no denying what she saw. This was for Aristedes. Alex wanted his father to hold him.

She reeled. Could it be Alex had recognized Aristedes, his blood calling to his? And what about Aristedes?

The first time Alex had done that, even when Aristedes had begun to succumb to Alex's tearful, heart-tugging demand, and even from afar, she'd seen how...unsettled he'd been. Her eyes clung to him now, feverishly trying to read his reaction. She could sense worry still. But it was of a different kind, something she'd never thought she'd see on Aristedes's face. Almost…trepidation.

He turned bemused eyes to her, letting her decide whether he could hold Alex or not, explaining his own worry. "I've never held a baby."

"Not even your brothers and sisters?" she whispered.

He shook his head. "No. I never had pets, either."

"He's no longer scary to hold." She decided to let Alex steer them both in this since she was totally lost, and Aristedes looked as out of his depth as she felt. She loosened her grasp on Alex, felt she was letting her heart go, trusting it to Aristedes.

Aristedes received the eager Alex with hands that visibly shook. As soon as the tiny yet strong body filled his large hands, they convulsed. Alex gave a squeak of protest.

Selene snapped a soothing hand to Alex, another to one of Aristedes's hands. "You don't need to hold on tight. He holds himself up perfectly now. You just cradle him, let him lean into your hold."

Aristedes nodded, looking poleaxed as he cautiously loosened his hold, as if he was still afraid Alex would spill out or come apart. Alex wriggled, made himself comfortable in Aristedes's power and started to explore him with avid glances and hands all over his father's face and chest.

"Hello, Alex." He transferred his gaze from Alex to her, shell-shocked traces still glittering in the eyes she could now see would be Alex's almost four decades into the future. "Shall I introduce myself, or will you do the honors?"

She couldn't have spoken if someone had demanded it of her at gunpoint. She gestured for him to go ahead.

Aristedes expanded his expansive chest on a huge breath. The movement raised and lowered Alex, which he found extremely entertaining, giggling and slamming both hands on Aristedes's chest, demanding he do it again.

Aristedes understood and did it again, before he began simulating the movement without breathing deep. Alex deciphered the difference and made his objections known with a sharp yelp, slapping Aristedes's chest as if commanding he move it once more.

Aristedes placed a hand on top of both of Alex's, holding them over his heart. "I'm not hyperventilating just because you think it's a fun game. Not a good start to our... acquaintance, for me to be dizzy and to be doing your bidding already."

Alex stilled, listening to Aristedes's deep, modulated voice, looking as if hypnotized into those eyes that Selene knew firsthand wielded mind-controlling powers. She was sure that if Alex knew how to say "yes, sir," he would have said it.

"Now that I have your attention, let me tell you who I am. I'm your father, Alex."

Selene's heart almost exploded from her ribs.

She had never thought she'd hear Aristedes say those words, let alone like this. And Alex...she could swear he understood. Why else did he give this sudden squee of delight?

"Your mother calls me Aristedes, or Sarantos." Aristedes went on. "Or both, if she's really mad at me. I want to be Aris to her. And Papa to you. How about you try this out for today?"

"He hasn't said anything yet." Selene heard her voice trembling. "Not real words, anyway."

Aristedes eyes moved to hers distractedly. "Too early?"

She coughed her incredulity. "You know nothing about kids for real, do you?"

He gave a tight shrug. "Right up till this moment, nothing at all, apart from the fact that they are scary and fragile and noisy and they take over a person's life."

She found a chuckle bursting on her lips. "That's all true. And how." She sobered a bit, looking her love at Alex. "They're also priceless and worth every bit of sacrifice and suffering."

"Not everyone thinks so."

She stilled at the darkness that came over Aristedes's face like an eclipse. Was he talking about himself?

Before she could wonder, question him, Alex turned to her, whimpering, eyes imploring.

She exhaled a ragged breath. "He wants breakfast. He always wakes up hungry."

"I do, too."

A wave of goose bumps stormed through her. She remembered how he woke up. Ravenous. For her, for food, then for her again...

She tamped down the urge to press against him, feel that vast hunger his body contained, the instant ignition she was capable of unleashing.

That wasn't why he was here, wasn't how it should be.

To bypass the moment of madness, she tried to take Alex from him. Both man and baby overrode her, Aristedes turning away a fraction while Alex nestled more securely into his arms, declaring his preference of vehicles.

"Turncoat!" she muttered as she pivoted, her heart sputtering with a crazy mixture of disappointment and delight.

Aristedes's sonorous, satisfied chuckles followed her all the way to the kitchen.

Once there, she gestured to Alex's high chair. Aristedes placed him there with all the care one might use to defuse a bomb.

He pulled back after he'd buckled Alex in and put his tray in place, all relieved triumph at this unprecedented achievement.

She smirked at him. "Since he wants you to hold him, you can do the rest of the morning 'honors.'"

Aristedes's eyes widened on something close to terror. "You mean you want me to *feed* him?"

She almost laughed at Aristedes's totally incongruous expression of helplessness and shock. "A scary new experience every second, eh? That's what everyday life with a baby is."

Aristedes shook his head, nodded, then his eyes moved down to her breasts, a mixture of hunger and bemusement entering the silver of his eyes. "You don't nurse him?"

Images of *his* head at her breasts, his lips suckling her nipples, exploded in her mind, flooded her body, her core.

She shook them off, handed him two of the food jars she'd prepared before she'd gone to bed. "You think I need to do that in the kitchen? But to answer your question, not anymore. He weaned himself, adamantly, at six months. He wants to *eat*."

Aristedes said nothing as Alex's impatient prodding made him concentrate on the alien chore. He dipped the small spoon into the pureed fruit mix, offered it tentatively to Alex. Alex lunged and inhaled the spoon's contents.

A laugh of surprise and delight rumbled deep in Aristedes's chest as he offered him more then more spoonfuls, all which met the same fate. "He certainly does want to eat."

She resisted the urge to run her fingers through the deep mahogany mane bent before her. "Remind you of someone?"

He turned his head to her, eyes crinkled with the first real smile she'd ever seen there. "We Sarantos men need our food."

"Alex is *not* a Sarantos."

Selene's heart convulsed with instant regret over her vehemence, at the deep, still darkness that crept into his eyes dousing the second-ago merriment.

"I meant biologically speaking," he finally acknowledged. "In all other ways, he's yours. A Louvardis."

She wondered how deep the need to make Alex a Sarantos had insinuated itself inside Aristedes. At this stage she could only believe he was too Greek, too male, that not being able to lay claim to what was his, "biologically speaking," hurt.

Nothing more was said as Alex polished off his food. In his enjoyment of the new experience of having Aristedes serving him, he hadn't picked up on the sudden tension between his parents. Still silent, Selene gestured for Aristedes to take him out of his high chair and follow her to another cross section of the everyday reality he'd wanted to witness and share.

Once in Selene's sunny, child-friendly sitting room, he placed Alex in his playpen. Alex made a beeline for his favorite toys, tackling playtime with the same determination his father attacked business projects.

Her Turkish Van cat, Apollo, woke up at their entry. Instead of dashing away at the sight of strangers as he usually did, he rose, stretched leisurely, and jumped off the couch and approached Aris in avid curiosity.

Aris purred encouragements to him and in moments had the unfriendly-but-to-her-and-Alex cat purring back in his hold.

After moments of fondling an ecstatic cat, Aristedes

put Apollo down. As the cat rushed to join Alex in play, Aristedes straightened and the vast space that she'd furnished in bright blues and greens seemed to shrink.

"Is Alex his real name or is it short for something else?"

She gulped a knot of emotion. "Alexandros."

Aristedes nodded, clearly approving. "He's nine months."

"Ten." He raised his eyes at that. "His doctor said developmentally, I should count him as a month less until after he passes the one-year mark. But so far he's actually ahead of the average curve."

Aristedes frowned. "He should be nine months."

She squared her shoulders, met his scowl with narrowing eyes. "Are you thinking he's not yours, after all?"

There was no hesitation. "I *know* he's mine. Not just because I felt it the moment I laid eyes on him, but because you would have told me, and delighted in telling me, if he wasn't."

She pulled herself to her full height. "I wouldn't have 'delighted' in doing any such thing. I'm not vindictive. And then, why should I have thought it would matter to you? It didn't occur to me you'd want to have anything to do with him."

He analyzed her affront for a long moment. Then a slight smile tugged at his lips. "Two more things corrected, then. On my side and yours. So you had him early. Why?"

She cocked her head, trying to even out her breathing, which kept going haywire at the unexpected reactions he continued hitting her with. "Why do women have premature babies?"

"I'm sure each does for a reason. What was yours?"

"I had a condition called placenta previa." His gaze

sharpened, inviting her to elaborate. "The placenta was too low and started bleeding. A week later, I went into premature labor."

"Was it painful, the…condition? The labor?"

"The condition, no, just painless bleeding. The labor was only bad in the last couple hours. Turned out I was in labor all day and dismissed the contractions, since it was too early."

His gaze filled with too many things to decipher.

"I wish I could have been there." Her heart lurched. Another silence stretched. Then that smile again softened the storms of his eyes. "But I'm here now."

That made her go mute, then babble. The one thing that had any context was when she offered him breakfast. He only dealt her another surprise, showing her that he was as ingenious in the kitchen as he was in the boardroom and bedroom.

After they'd taken their trays back to the sitting room and he set about wiping his plate clean, he looked at her. "So how do you usually spend your weekends?"

She swallowed a mouthful of the delicious smoked salmon and vegetable crepe he'd made. "How do you?"

He shrugged. "I don't have weekends."

"Figures. But then neither did I, before Alex."

"Did you work all through your pregnancy?"

"Yes."

That made him raise his eyes from his plate. "You didn't eat enough. You are thinner than you used to be."

"You don't approve?"

His eyes slid down her body, leaving her in no doubt how much he did approve and gasping with a sudden flare of the arousal he always had simmering inside her before he said, "Only that you're not taking as good care of yourself as you should."

She tore her gaze away from his, busied herself with swallowing without choking on the cocktail of explosive reactions he incited inside her. "I had a lot on my mind, and since I had Alex, far more to worry about and do."

"What do you worry about?" His question was deceptively casual, but she felt the intensity of interest vibrating in it.

"Everything. That's what being a mother is all about, it seems."

"Tell me."

His simple yet imperative demand made her realize how acutely she'd wanted to share these details. But there'd been no one to share them with. Now he was here. And he wanted, seemed to even *need*, to share. Floodgates opened inside her.

"I constantly worry about things that never crossed my mind before, or things I never thought were worrisome in the least. I *invent* worries, and each can become an obsession. When I left Alex to go back to work, I'd work myself up with imaginary scenarios, and if Eleni didn't pick up after the first two rings, I was tearing down to my car. The first time she didn't answer I drove like a maniac out of the building, left my car when I got caught in a traffic jam and ran here."

He was sitting at the edge of her plush sofa by now. "Why didn't she answer?"

"She was giving Alex a bath and he makes quite a racket. She didn't think to check her phone afterward for missed calls. Since the…episode, she says she keeps her phone with her even if she's in the shower in her own home."

His compressed lips twitched. "I would have done something drastic, too."

Conversation flowed after that. About every momentous and inconsequential thing that had happened once she'd discovered her pregnancy. Aristedes seemed insatiable in his need to know everything. And when there were silences, they were not tense and uncomfortable. They were companionable, content, communicative.

She couldn't credit it. She'd never expected rapport to flow between them. But it did. And that was the part between them. What passed between Alex and Aristedes shook her even more. Alex was beside himself with delight to have him around. While Aristedes stunned her with his eagerness for Alex, with his handling of him with such instinctive insight and sensitivity, such patience, firmness and affection.

The day flowed. They puttered around the house doing whatever she and Alex did always alone, together. Aristedes brought new dimensions to their activities, turned playing with Alex, giving him a bath, dressing him, feeding him, putting him down for his nap into far more fun, not to mention more efficient endeavors.

She let him treat her to a leisurely and delicious lunch like he had breakfast, then after Alex woke up from his afternoon nap ravenous again, they fed him and she served tea.

Two hours before what she'd told Aristedes was Alex's bedtime, he suddenly stood up, said he had to go do something. Alex made a tearful, vocal protest when he realized Aristedes was leaving, but Aristedes soothed him, promising he'd be right back. Alex seemed to understand, to believe him, and got reengaged in crawling around, exploring the condo under her supervision.

After the first half hour passed, she began to think Aristedes wouldn't return.

Maybe he'd put up with as much mundane normality as he could stomach for this lifetime, had decided he'd forgo being anything to either her or Alex, would call to tell her some business emergency had cropped up or something.

After an hour passed, she was certain he wouldn't come back.

Then her doorbell rang.

She flew, hating herself for her uncontrollable eagerness, her dread of opening the door to find someone else there.

Her legs almost buckled when she found it *was* Aristedes.

This time he had flowers and two gift-wrapped boxes with him.

With an intense glance, he handed her the flowers. She took them, her mind spinning, watched him walk up to Alex, who met him with even more enthusiasm than the first time.

Aristedes went down on his haunches beside him and unwrapped the boxes, all the while explaining what he'd gotten him. One box contained an animated activity book. The second had a toy made of colorful, pliable plastic loops.

As Alex began pawing the activity book in captive fascination, Aristedes looked up at her, gesturing at the other toy. "These can be refrigerated for a soothing teether."

He'd noticed. That Alex was chewing on everything. This was new, since his first teeth had come out with no discomfort. She'd just noticed it herself, had made a note to buy him some teethers. But Aristedes had noticed he had these missing from his toys. And judged what else he'd be interested in that he didn't have.

He'd gotten her an incredible assortment of lilies, her absolute favorites. He'd realized that, too, from her mugs and trays and coasters.

The gifts weren't expensive. But they were…just right.

She didn't remember what she said, or what they did

until Alex, who'd been playing contentedly at their feet, suddenly lay on his side and was asleep in seconds.

"That's his new trick," she said when Aristedes looked at her with surprise and a tinge of worry in his eyes. "After eight months of keeping me awake at night."

His worry drained to be replaced by something so… soft. "A merciful trick. He's enough of a handful during the day."

She nodded and he rose, pulled her up to her feet, bent and picked up Alex then walked with her to the nursery to put him in his crib.

They were walking down the corridor afterward, feet away from her bedroom door, when he stopped, looked down at her.

To ameliorate the unbearable intensity of the moment, she said, "Thanks for the gifts again…Aris." His eyes flared at hearing the name he'd expressed as his desire to hear on her lips. She forced the rest out. "You didn't have to."

"I wanted to. I'm glad you and Alex enjoyed my choices."

"They were very…astute."

"And I'm nothing if not astute, eh?"

She didn't want him to think she was implying it was another manipulation, wanted to wipe that sardonic twist off his mouth. "That wasn't a veiled dig."

She succeeded. He smiled, all traces of disappointment evaporating. "No. You don't do veiled anything. It's all out there in the open, full blast, in my face with you."

Before she could say any more, he caught her to him. She melted in his arms on the spot, like a candle in an inferno.

He swept her up, took her from gravity's hold into his, took her lips, over and over, in clinging, will-draining kisses, then rumbled inside her trembling depths, "Thank *you* for the gift of today, Selene."

Her head spun, her thoughts tangled, her heart splashed and spilled, her body ached, begged, wept.

When she thought he'd sweep her around, take her to her bedroom and end her torment, he raised his head, straightened.

"I think this means I'm granted another day," he groaned as he let her slide down his body, put her on her feet. He held her for one last shuddering moment then turned and walked away.

Before he closed the condo's door behind him, he smoldered at her over his shoulder. "Till tomorrow, *kala mou*."

Six

Selene spent the night in an unremitting fever.

Every moment of the day Aris had spent with her, with them, kept replaying in a loop inside her head until she felt her vital circuitry overheating, melting.

Aris—as she suddenly could only think of him—could have stayed the night if he'd wanted. He must have known he could have made her beg him to stay. But he hadn't. Why?

He'd wanted to. At least, he'd wanted sex. Her body pounded its demand for him again as it relived feeling the daunting hardness of his desire against her molten core. Yet he'd still walked away. She could think of only one reason why.

This experiment he was conducting didn't include sex as one of its parameters. As she'd said more than once, nothing to prove in that arena. Sexually, they were compatible, explosively so.

But…were they? Maybe he responded like that to any reasonably attractive female who had the hots for him. As for her reaction, it must be what he got from all women. He'd intimated that what they shared was special, but men did say things like that in their efforts to get resistant women to agree to their casual arrangements. But now, as he'd also made it clear, things were no longer that simple. Alex complicated matters. Now casual sex wasn't in Aris's best interests, or those of his "test."

By the time the first strands of dawn filtered through her bedroom window, her turmoil had reached its zenith.

And she decided. She'd call him first thing in the morning. Tell him she wasn't continuing this experiment. If he wanted to continue to see Alex, they could come to an arrangement. If the arrangement worked, and in a couple years' time, if he lasted that long and proved to be a constant and positive presence in Alex's life, they would discuss making Alex his legally.

She didn't want to be included in this test. She had no doubt the part concerning *them* would either collapse dramatically or expire gradually. And she didn't enter into endeavors she knew were doomed to failure, no matter the temptation.

At 8:00 a.m. sharp, she phoned him.

Seconds later, she heard a no-frills, classic ringtone. On the other side of her condo's door.

Her heart gave one violent boom before it stumbled into a mad gallop.

Aris. He was on her doorstep. He'd come back.

She expected him to see her number, reject the call, ring the doorbell. But since when did he ever do the expected?

The phone she still had clamped to her ear clicked and his velvet-night voice poured right into her brain. "*Kalimera,* Selene. I hope you had a better night than the one I had."

"If you had a terrible night, we have a stalemate."

A dark chuckle, male smugness made audible, purred into her ear, vibrated along her already-strung-tight nerves, made her palms itch, made her press her thighs together. "And you're going to punish me by leaving me standing on your doorstep?"

So he knew she knew he was outside her door. She wouldn't ask how he knew, wouldn't bother pretending she hadn't known. "If you think you deserve punishment, you evidently think you're the reason for my terrible night."

"I *know* you're the reason for mine." Suddenly his voice dipped into a whisper potent enough to blow a woman's hormonal fuses. "I wouldn't mind you punishing me, though. In fact, the very idea is appealing to me more by the second. But only if you do it…firsthand. Open the door and dish it out, *kala mou*."

On top of everything he had to go Greek on her and call her "my beauty" and in that devastatingly sensual way, too. How would she tell him of her resolution now?

She had to, though. Somehow. She should just open the door and get it over with.

She rose on jellified legs, teetered to the door, opened it.

And Aris was standing there, overwhelming all over again in a casual-chic silk suit the color of his eyes.

This time, he had a woman with him.

She looked her confusion from him to the woman and back.

He only singed her with one of those smiles he was suddenly generous with. "Selene, I want you to meet Caliope."

Selene looked dazedly at the stunningly beautiful woman she judged to be a couple years younger than her, who was clinging to his arm as if she was afraid to get blown away in an unexpected hurricane if she didn't hang on tight enough.

She was Selene's height, but far more curvaceous. Her skin boasted the most perfect sun-kissed tan she'd ever seen, looked incandescent against her white blouse and cardigan, also showed off hair streaked a hundred shades of bronze, caramel and gold and the most intense azure eyes that didn't belong to a cat.

She started to nod at the woman, not sure what to think, what to say. The woman let go of Aris, extended a hand to her. Selene took her hand only for the woman to pull her closer, looking at her avidly.

Then she blurted out, "Is it true? You have Aristedes's son?"

Selene's eyes swung up to Aris. He'd told her? Whoever she was?

But she couldn't even accuse him of breaching her trust. She hadn't asked him to keep it a secret. Why had she thought he would? It might be in his best interest to expose her, to force her to acknowledge him as Alex's father.

As if reading her anxiety and suspicions, Aris gave her a placating glance. "If you want a secret kept, you trust it to Caliope." Aris looked down into Caliope's suddenly sheepish eyes. "I bet even I haven't developed as unreadable a poker face and demeanor as my youngest sister—when she wants."

Sister?

He looked back at Selene. "Since Eleni isn't coming today, I drafted Caliope into babysitting Alex while we're out."

"Out?" Selene echoed, her confusion deepening.

Caliope rolled her eyes. "You didn't know, huh? Should have guessed he's drafting you into an outing, too."

Aristedes raised a sardonic eyebrow at his sister. "I

drafted you only until you knew what this was all about, then I couldn't walk fast enough to keep up with you as you zoomed to my car."

"You bet I'd zoom, when my oldest brother comes telling me he has a ten-month-old baby, when I didn't even know he was capable of procreating…" She winced, bit her lip. "I didn't mean it that way, of course, since anyone looking at you will know you are, *that* way. I *meant* I always thought you weren't exactly human—"

As Caliope gasped, then spluttered inaudible self-abuse at herself, Aris's remaining eyebrow joined his raised one. "Always nice to know for sure what my 'family' thinks of me."

"You know we love you, in spite of everything we think of you—" Caliope stopped again, grimaced, then groaned, "Okay, I'll shut up now. Preferably forever."

Aris gave a huff, twisted his lips at his sister's red-faced distress. "Now that we've had that character-assassinating promo campaign in front of Selene, the mother of my miracle child, let's hope we get invited over her threshold."

"You mean she keeps you just outside, like a vampire…?"

Aris looked whimsically into Selene's no doubt still-stricken eye as Caliope choked into chagrined self-chastisement. "First, I'm a different species, then a species incapable of procreating with humans, now we get to the specifics about what kind of inhuman entity I am. Will you at least prove to this know-it-all that she got…which one wrong?"

"Her assessment isn't far from the truth," Selene heard herself croak as she stepped back, wordlessly inviting them to come in. "You do suck the lifeblood out of rivals."

"So you think so, too? But you couldn't resist him, huh? That actually supports my theory."

As Caliope eagerly asked her corroboration, Selene

revised her estimate of her age. Caliope felt younger than she'd first thought, probably in her early twenties, making the difference between her age and Aris's more than fifteen years. She hadn't known he had siblings that much younger. Or that he'd treat one with such patience and indulgence.

What else didn't she know about him?

"Between the two of you, who needs smear campaigns?" Aris sighed as he watched Selene lead Caliope to the sitting area. He came to stand before them as they sat down, the very image of masculine grandeur as he looked in the direction of her sleeping quarters. "I think it's time we brought Alex into this delightful meeting. He, at least, doesn't think I'm a monster."

"He'll probably wake up now," Selene said, feeling bad that she'd collaborated with his sister in "smearing" him. Not that he sounded hurt or anything. It seemed he included her in his forbearance. But then, he had said he'd enjoy her "punishing" him...

"Great!" Caliope exclaimed. "I can't believe I actually have a nephew from Aristedes! And I get to spend a day with him!"

"But I can't leave Alex!" Selene protested, feeling this development snowballing, having no idea how to stop it.

Caliope put a reassuring, exquisitely manicured hand on her forearm. "You can. With my two older sisters married and breeding like crazy, they provided me with all sorts of kids to babysit. I'm an old hand at it by now." She hesitated. "Though we're talking about Aristedes's son here." Then she seemed to get worried. "Maybe he'll be too much for me to handle!"

Selene, who didn't want anyone babysitting Alex, especially not to go out with his father, still took exception to Caliope's dawning anxiety.

Before she could defend Alex, Aris barked a laugh.

"I assure you, Caliope, Alex isn't as monstrous as his father."

"I didn't mean that!" Caliope rolled her eyes and groaned. "Maybe I'll just record *that* statement, and put it on auto replay." Her embarrassment deepened as she looked at Selene. "Really, I meant no offense to your baby, since that would reflect on you, too." A second's pause. "Okay, I'm babbling, but it's not every day the Sarantos chieftain comes confiding in me and asking—insert gasps of shock and fainting thuds here—for my help."

Aris looked at Caliope sardonically. "And you're working as hard as you can to make it the last time."

"Oh, no!" Caliope gasped. "I'll shut up now, I swear. And I'll be your best babysitter ever, you'll have to use me again."

"And *that* will be up to Selene." Aris turned his eyes to her. "Can I go fetch Alex now?"

Selene's first instinct was to cry out that *she* would. But she held back. He was Alex's father. And even if she wasn't ready, not by a long shot, to declare that to the world and didn't think one day in Alex's company qualified Aris to be his father for the rest of his life, he'd proved that he could be trusted with Alex. In the short term. In the long run... *that* remained to be seen.

She nodded her consent. And her heart turned over in her chest—at the unadulterated eagerness and elation that blazed on his face as he zoomed away, homing in on Alex's nursery as if she'd had him on a leash and had just released him.

Caliope giggled. "Whoa! Is that my oldest brother?" Selene didn't know she was smiling until Caliope's next words wiped the satisfied expression off her face. "And if it is, for how long?"

Caliope was still kicking herself by the time Aris walked

back. It was only the sight of an adorably sleep-rumpled if gleeful Alex in his arms that brought her apologies to an abrupt halt.

She rose, an expression of open wonder seizing her stunning face. "Oh. My. God! So human cloning has been achieved!"

"Alex, this pretty lady with the big mouth is your aunt Caliope." Aris chuckled as Caliope bounced toward them, all uncontainable delight. Alex inspected her with interest as his father went on explaining. "This means she's my kid sister, even though it seems that's not one of her favorite facts."

Caliope gasped, her tan darkening with mortification. Aris gave her a quick wink, as if to tell her he was okay with it, had never expected anything else.

Again, to Selene's total amazement, it seemed as if Alex understood his father's every word. She could swear he would have nodded if he knew how. In lieu of a nod, he gave a loud squeal and giggled, burying his face shyly in his father's endless chest.

"Can I hold you now, Alex?" Caliope extended her arms to him. "I'll drop dead of cuteness deprivation if I don't!"

And again, Alex stunned Selene. He gave a suspicious whimper as that beautiful angel reached for him, buried deeper into his father's hold. This after he'd thrown himself at the intimidating juggernaut he had for a father at first sight.

Aris kissed the top of Alex's head, put his finger below his chin, bringing his gaze up to his. "Now, now, Alex. She's not the monster she looks." He gave Caliope a bedeviling glance. "She's nice—" his goading rose a notch higher as he crossed his fingers "—and loves kids. But a word of warning, she doesn't let adorable tykes like you get away with much. I'm taking your mama out, and I don't want her worrying about you the entire time. So be a good boy, don't give your auntie Caliope any hassles and let her entertain you. But I promise we'll be back before your bedtime. Deal?"

Alex, who seemed totally taken with his father's voice and words, squeaked a merry acknowledgment.

Aris kissed his forehead, leaned him closer to Caliope. "Now let's be nice to your auntie and let her hold you before she hyperventilates."

This time, Alex pitched into Caliope's waiting arms.

Caliope began chattering to him, taking him away as if escaping with a gift before its giver changed his mind. Alex seemed fine with it, evidently taking his father's vouching for her to heart and promptly began examining her face and hair and accessories.

Aris turned to Selene. "Why don't you get dressed while Alex and Caliope get acquainted?"

"Why do you want to go out?" She shook her spinning head. "You're both welcome to stay with us today."

"No. We need to have some time alone."

"Okay, then," she countered, floundering. "How about after Alex goes to bed? Caliope can babysit him without incident while he sleeps. I have a ton of series DVDs for her to watch while we're out catching a late dinner or movie or something."

"Do you have *Lost?*" Caliope perked up from across the room. "And *House?* And *Star Trek?*"

"I have the complete seasons of *House,*" Selene said, hoping this would be the alternative to this "outing" right now, and she'd find a way to tell him of her resolution before it came to pass. "And *Star Trek: The Original Series* and *The Next Generation.*"

Caliope whooped in excitement. "I'll sleep over if you like!"

"No, she wouldn't like," Aris said emphatically.

Caliope grunted in protest, and Selene glared at him. "I'll make the decisions for myself, thank you. And I don't want to go out with you."

There, she'd said it.

Maddeningly, he gave her one of those part indulgent, part devouring smiles that rocked her to her foundations. "You do. But you seem to have decided it's better not to give me a full test run after all." He'd read her mind! "But I'll hold you to your word to give it to me, demand the extra day I earned."

She swallowed. "I never gave you my word, and *you* declared you earned an extra day, not I."

"Your word was implicit when you let me have yesterday, so was your agreement to my declaration when you didn't contest it."

"I wasn't in much of a condition to contest anything in both situations."

His gaze stilled on her, all traces of humor disappearing. "Don't fight me, Selene. There's no need for you to."

"There's plenty of need. It's what people do when they find themselves being taken over. And you're the master of takeovers."

Her accusation slid right off him. He shrugged. "I'm only making sure I'm given a full and fair test. You know a couple sides to me, the businessman and the lover. This is the best way we can discover if there's more to me than that. And whether we have more than unquenchable lust and an incredible baby in common."

"Listen…about this first commonality…" she started, and he pulled her into his arms.

His lips captured her still-open ones, seared her with his hunger, evaporating every intention of telling him to leave her out of the equation along with every objection and trepidation.

Time expanded, her senses warped. She thought she heard a feminine voice exclaim "Woohoo" and a baby shrieking in delight. She knew she should be mortified, fuzzily thought she'd have to be so after he ended this mind-blanking pleasure.

Then he did. He raised his head enough to look down at her. She vaguely knew she was still clinging to him as if she'd always needed and would always need his support.

He bent for another kiss as if compelled to before he withdrew, ran a possessive finger down her cheek. "*What* about that first commonality?"

And she knew there was no way she could tell him she didn't want more of him, with him, and mean it. She didn't know where this could lead, had a feeling nowhere good, but it was no use. This was unstoppable, what she craved from him was overpowering. She had to capitulate to its demand. For now.

She pulled back from his arms, congratulated herself on turning around and tossing him a glance over her shoulder without falling over. "Fine. I will give you today, too. But anything else, you check with me first."

"Yes, ma'am." He riddled her vision with another smile then drawled, "And wear a skirt."

Her knees knocked.

"I will when *you* do," she bit off.

She strode off fuming, her heat raging higher as his guffaws followed her all the way to her bedroom.

Selene wore a skirt.

Technically. As part of a dress. And no, she hadn't succumbed to Aris's demand. It was the most flattering daytime outfit she had in a wardrobe made of lawyerlike formal wear or mom-with-drooling-baby casual clothes. She wasn't going out with that paragon of male beauty and elegance looking less than her absolute best.

And she was sticking to that story.

Aris had smoldered his satisfaction at seeing her, poured leisurely lust along the curve of her hips in the flowing dress the color of her eyes, down the smoothness of her panty-hosed legs to her platform shoes. He hadn't put his triumph into words, though. Wise man. She would have hurt him if he had.

But throughout the day, he kept saying, in so many creative ways, how edible and sublime she looked. She discovered she couldn't get enough of his praise, hungered for it with the same constant ache she did for him.

Thinking he had an itinerary planned, she was stunned when he told her he was putting himself in her hands. He'd never seen the city, wanted her to take him to the places that had witnessed her favorite experiences and formed chunks of her memories.

From then on, she had a constant lump in her throat. At the willingness with which he agreed to anything she suggested, the wholeheartedness in which he followed her as she took him walking along the pier, cycling across the Brooklyn Bridge and riding in a horse-drawn carriage, feeding birds and having a picnic beneath a gigantic oak tree in Central Park.

Hours later, after lunch, they'd just finished the hot cocoa he'd run two miles round-trip for when he pulled her to him, encompassed her back with the warmth and comfort of his expansive chest and covered her with his jacket.

She melted against him, inhaling the intoxicating amalgam of his freshness, vigor and unique brand of distilled testosterone. He rubbed his jaw on the top of her head, murmuring enjoyment, too.

"Thank you for showing me your city, Selene," he rumbled against her temple. "This, along with yesterday, was the best time I remember ever having."

Her heart expanded so fast, so hard, she felt it would burst. She twisted to look up into his eyes. "I can't believe you've been here so many times and never been anywhere."

"I never had anyone I wanted to be anywhere with. Now I do."

The tightness in her chest, behind her eyes, became unbearable. That sounded scarily wonderful. He sounded terribly lonely.

As if hearing her thoughts, he sighed. "I never felt I was missing anything, though." That unfurled the tension inside her. She was glad he hadn't been suffering in his voluntary segregation. "Now I know I was."

She pressed deeper into his hold, as if to absorb any pain he was feeling in retrospect. "I thought I knew the city I've lived in all my life. But experiencing it with you, I feel I saw it through new eyes, with a combination of your fresh perspective and—"

A bird flapped inches away, making her swallow the rest of her words. Good thing it had. Saying *the beauty of seeing it with you* was too premature to feel, let alone admit.

They shared a long, tranquil silence, even though, for her, it was charged with heart-clogging confusion.

Suddenly he inhaled. "Until we settle things, I think we should keep this all between us."

She raised her eyes to him. Her expression must have betrayed her hesitation about how to take his request. He rushed to add, "I don't want to introduce the volatile element of your family with their personal misconceptions and business tensions. They'd have nothing but a negative role right now."

Truth be told, she wanted nothing more than to keep her family out of this. Still, when he'd been the one to spell it out, a frisson of disappointment and suspicion had zapped through her. The reasons would fill a book with the contrariness only Aris incited in her, the stupid insecurities and paradoxes only he unearthed.

She suddenly felt the need to be away from him. At her first wriggle, he let her go. She started to rise, and he was on his feet in an impossibly fluid move, helping her up.

She walked ahead. He followed, caught up with her.

Suddenly he jumped in the air.

She blinked in surprise. He'd caught a Frisbee that had flown their way. Then she heard the giggles. She followed their trajectory to half a dozen coeds, all cute and in clinging tops and skimpy shorts.

He handed it to the buxom blonde who advanced on him, all suggestiveness. He looked down at her and her group with that mild amusement of the supremely confident male he was, said something that had them howling with laughter.

The incident took no more than two minutes. But it was enough to plunge her mood into frost.

They walked on in silence, she wondering how she'd thought a man like him could have been lonely. Or that she was in any way different to him from the hordes who panted after him.

"You do that on autopilot, don't you?"

He raised an eyebrow.

"Enthrall women," she elaborated.

"I can say the same about you, with men," he shot back.

"I don't affect men anywhere near the way you affect women."

His eyes narrowed, raising the heat of his contention. "You mean you didn't notice the dropped jaws littering the city in your wake today? I'm almost sorry I asked you to wear a skirt. Boosting your femininity was definitely overkill."

"Oh, come on. Men aren't throwing themselves at me."

"No, since men need to be invited to make a move. Women have the luxury of 'throwing' themselves without being accused of harassment."

"You mean you feel harassed by women's pursuit? You don't invite it? Don't allow it, at least?"

"You think I invited or allowed it? Just now?"

"No. I mean in general. Your reputation as a playboy is legend."

"More of an urban myth. But if we're trading misconceptions, I'd recite the incidents where you left lasting devastation in the ranks of the far more fragile male population."

She almost snorted. "Men are more fragile? Which planet are you living on?"

"This one, which you evidently haven't truly inhabited if you don't realize that women are *far* more resilient than men."

This gave her pause. "So the stories about you aren't true?"

"I was never promiscuous. I never had the inclination."

"But you had plenty of one-night stands."

"According to reports? But contrary to them, I can actually count the times I've had sex since I became sexually active at fifteen. In almost twenty-five years, I haven't had near as many women. What turned out to be mostly one-night stands for me wasn't because I wanted a new flavor the next time, but because I didn't find *that single taste* I wanted to have over and over. In fact, most of my sexual encounters were aborted because…the taste didn't appeal to me." He looked steadily into her eyes, wiping her mind clean of her preconceptions of him, installing the version he was relaying. "The other major reason no man should think of being promiscuous even if he had the indiscriminate taste to be so is that women are people. Very complex and complicated people."

That made her hoot. "Oh, thanks for that piece of revolutionary thinking!"

His huff was sardonic. "I mean a promiscuous man thinks women are pastimes, thinks he indulges himself only with the no-strings variety. But there's no such thing. Women always have strings and require effort and time. I never had either to spare. So I didn't. I only ever accepted invitations from those who made it clear to me what those strings were, things I could give without infringing on my priorities."

She hated hearing him talk about his sex life with such brutal honesty, yet was relieved it hadn't been quite as she'd imagined. "Material things?"

"I offered gifts to anyone, not only sexual partners, who I thought would appreciate it, and because I can. None of them was a favor for sharing my bed. Though the bed sharing here is metaphorical. I never did sleepovers."

"You did with me," she whispered.

His pupils suddenly engulfed the silver of his eyes. "And I wanted to keep on doing it. But you skipped out on me."

"I didn't know what to do next. Thought I'd let you decide."

There. She'd admitted her insecurity.

His face froze. "You could have left me some indication that you didn't think it the biggest mistake of your life."

She bit her lip to stop its trembling. "You could have called me, if even only to say thanks for the good time. I might have let you know I wasn't against repeating it."

Silence reverberated in the field of tension that engulfed them.

At last he exhaled heavily. "So we both made a mistake. And lost ourselves eighteen months."

"I'm sure you found…alternatives during that time."

He gave her an irritable glance. "What for? Whatever little satisfaction other women used to offer no longer existed."

Everything stilled inside her.

"Are you telling me you haven't…since me?"

"No," he simply said. "Have you, since me?"

She bit her lip again. "Uh, if you didn't notice, I was busy being pregnant and having a baby."

That mind-reading focus of his sharpened on her face. "And those are the only reasons you didn't…date other men?"

"No," she admitted as straightforwardly as he had. "But I can't believe it was the same for you."

His gaze grew so deep, she felt it penetrate her marrow. And that was before he said, "Why can't you? I found no point in having less than what I had with you. Not when you were the taste I've always looked for and never stopped craving."

After that admission sent her spiraling into turmoil, as if by unspoken agreement to lay off the soul-baring discussions, they exchanged nothing of consequence for the rest of the day.

Then it was time to see Alex before his bedtime.

Back at her condo, they found Caliope and Alex getting along like a house on fire. Alex shrieked his welcome at their sight, rushed to slobber on each of them equally.

Aris and Caliope stayed far beyond Alex's bedtime, and Aris again cooked for his "ladies." Caliope could barely speak with shock when she saw him heading to the kitchen. Then with each mouthful of the heavenly soufflé he'd prepared, she kept saying how the foundation of her life had been irreversibly shaken.

Aris received her amazement with an enigmatic smile, one that had Selene itching to know just what stories it was hiding.

At one o'clock, Aris pulled Caliope up to leave.

They went into Alex's room first. Selene's heart twisted as Aris lovingly kissed the tiny sleeping replica of himself, almost asked him to stay with him, with her. With them.

But no matter how incredible the past two days had been, that step was far too premature.

At the door, Aris stood aside as Selene and Caliope hugged and planned future get-togethers, with Caliope gushing over the perfect day she'd had not only with Alex but with her, and most of all, with the oldest brother she was discovering anew.

He then let Caliope precede him to the elevators before waving at Selene and turning away.

She stared after him, disappointment detonating inside her.

But he took only one step away before retracing it, coming to stand before her, his hands bunched at his sides.

"No kiss good-night this evening, just so you don't go to work feeling as bad as I did this morning and make people bankrupt or send them to prison."

Relief crashed through her. He was holding back for her.

He suddenly groaned, took her hand, raised it to his lips. "Do I get another day, *kala mou?*"

And she could only whisper a tremulous, "Yes."

They didn't get another day.

All they got during the next two weeks were sporadic hours. She saw Aris when she finished work, *if* his own business released him from its shackles. Which it didn't the next two weekends.

But seeing less of him made her savor their time together more. She surrendered to the wonder of discovering him, learning things she'd never hoped to find in him, or with anyone else.

Then, on Friday, he told her he'd arrive at seven. He showed up at eleven, long after Alex had been in bed.

Her heart constricted again at finding him looking progressively more tired. Tonight he also seemed fed up, on edge.

The moment he sat down, his phone rang.

He apologized to her, walked to her veranda to take the call. She heard him growling with escalating aggression. She watched him from the kitchen as he came inside, flung the phone on the couch then strode with barely suppressed anger to her bathroom.

He came out with his hair wet. Seemed he'd needed to douse his head in cooling water.

She finally made her presence known, her heart twisting in her chest with the need to alleviate his tension.

He turned to her with a bleak tide turning his eyes black.

Then he muttered, "It's no use, Selene. This is not working."

Seven

"I-it isn't?"

Selene heard her strangled rasp, didn't know how it had been produced, let alone formulated words. Everything inside her had been flash frozen by Aris's declaration.

She watched him, the numbness of dread spreading as he shook his head, his bleakness deepening. "I hoped it would, that I could make it work, but no, it certainly isn't."

She couldn't think. Couldn't feel or let anything sink in.

But he was driving the icicles deeper into her heart. "I was a fool to think I could arrange my schedule to have enough time to be with you. And that was when I didn't know about Alex and the kind of time commitment he'd require."

He was giving up on them already.

He was telling her it was over. Before it really began.

No. He couldn't be. He'd seemed to want this to work

so much. And they'd been doing so well. So they hadn't continued as they'd begun. But they could organize themselves better. If they worked at it, they had the potential to become what those first two days had promised they could be. Happy to be with each other.

But she gazed into the twin thundercloud storms of his eyes and knew. He meant it. He was ending them.

He'd made his decision. And nothing would talk him out of it.

"I have to get away or I'll do something drastic." He ran spastic fingers through the thick locks of his damp hair, dug them into his scalp as if to defuse a pressure that would crush his skull. "I thought I'd take things slow, buy time, until I figured out how to make things work, with either everyone involved coming out winners, or at least suffering the least damage possible."

So he'd been factoring in damages. But even with worst outcomes accounted for, he already thought it wasn't working, was so at the end of his tether he wanted only to get away from them?

Up till two weeks ago, she'd been certain this would be his reaction to any personal closeness or responsibility. That he'd feel suffocated, would become contemptuous of, even disgusted with, those who needed him. She'd believed that Aris…Aristedes Sarantos was born to be a conqueror, never a nurturer.

But he'd showed her he had so much more to him than she'd thought. Things she couldn't have dreamed of.

He'd given her a glimpse of…perfection.

Had he discovered it would take more than he was prepared to provide in the long run, so he was cutting things short, before the damages entered the level of the unacceptable?

She should be thankful that he'd discovered this early, that he was being honest.

She wasn't. She only…hurt. Far more than she'd thought she would. She knew anger would come later. At herself. For letting him override her better judgment, for being so weak that she'd risked an injury she'd been almost certain she'd sustain.

But he probably thought, with her initial resistance and cynicism, that she'd been wading as superficially as he'd been, hadn't invested enough yet to feel any loss.

Unaware of her condition, he was bent on making his point. "When I told everyone involved in the current negotiations war that I was postponing my decision, that I will resume talks in a month's time, all hell broke loose. Instead of making everyone relax and take things slower, they think I'm going to orchestrate some unheard-of coup. Now everyone is pursuing me for any hint they can get out of me, any assurance for a piece of the action or at least shelter from the fallout when I finally make my move."

She blinked dazedly. "You're talking about the U.S. Navy contract?" The contract Louvardis wanted to oust him of.

He gritted his teeth, muttered, "What else. It seems my reputation is too established that no one will consider I mean it when I say I'm postponing making offers because I'm not ready to make any. They all think this is a maneuver to pull the rug out from under whomever I've decided to eliminate. Now, instead of laying off, they believe the world is ending, when all I want is one damn month to think things through. Or not to think, for once."

What did that have to do with deciding they were not working?

"Your brothers are behind the rabid reactions. They put their threat into action and are openly backing the Di Giordanos for a builder, and everyone who stands to lose a dime if I'm eliminated is chasing me like it's a matter of life or death."

She shook her head, tried to adjust her mind-set from the intensely personal to the purely business. "I almost have the draft we talked about done. My brothers will revise their stance if you offer it to them."

He'd already said he couldn't risk her involvement in his battle with her brothers. Not at the cost of having them suspect what was going on between them. He'd said he'd find another way around their adamant refusal to deal with him. But if things had gone this bad, this soon, maybe he'd reconsider.

He shut his eyes, opened them. She found them roiling with finality. "No. I have far more to lose by this maneuver than anything I stand to gain. For the moment I've made sure they can't move without me making a move first. So I'll leave things hanging, until I decide how to deal with it. Right now, for the first time ever, I can't see a viable course of action. And the way I'm feeling, if I'm pushed, it will be everyone's funeral."

Having her and Alex in his life for two weeks had plunged him into such turmoil? They should be in some record book as the ones who'd caused the iceberg Aristedes Sarantos to lose his cool. And he wanted to get away as fast as possible to regain it.

She turned. She had to, to breathe. She couldn't, as long as she saw the end of her foolish hopes in his eyes. "Then do what you always do—act only when you have everything planned to the last detail. As for us, we were an experiment. Failing it was always the probable outcome."

A shock wave of silence and stillness emanated from him, almost knocked her over.

At length, he rasped in a voice like a saw cutting steel, "What are you talking about?"

She pretended to busy herself with pouring the herbal tea she'd prepared for them. "If it's not working, it isn't. Best thing to do is to move on. Good thing we found this out early."

He moved. She barely saw him in her peripheral vision, but he filled her senses. She bit down on a keen of screaming tension as he came to stand before her. She kept her eyes averted, felt nothing but the waves of his power buffeting her.

Then he grated, "You think I meant that *we* are not working?"

His vehemence forced her eyes up. "What else?"

"I meant this!" He flung his hand toward the phone that was ringing again. "It rings at all hours. And I can't turn it off because if I do, they'll do anything to find me, and I don't want them following me here. *Theos,* Selene—you thought…"

He stopped, his eyes blazing, his Adam's apple working.

Then he suddenly clamped her shoulders in convulsive hands. "How could you think that? I'm at my wit's end only because this is interfering with my ability to be with you and Alex. This…*intrusion* is what isn't working, what I have to end."

As soon as the blow of relief almost buckled her legs, another of realization wiped it away, made them rigid again. "But *that*—" she nodded at the phone that was ringing again "—can't end. It's your *life.*"

"No," he said. "This is my biggest war yet, and I can't fight it properly because it involves your family, because I can't bring *us* into it and because on account of it, I'm unable to be what I need to be for you and Alex."

She shook her head again. "But there will always be bigger wars. This *is* your life, and if dealing with it stops you from being whatever you want to be for us, it always will."

His eyes grew burning in their urgency. "No, it won't. We don't have an established relationship. I'm new to this, am just learning what it takes to have others in my life. We are testing me, and I can't be fairly tested under these conditions. At this stage, it's setting me up for failure, and I can't afford to fail. That is why I need to be away from it all."

She tried to step back, to escape the renewed confusion. He wouldn't let her, clamped her flesh tighter. "I didn't mean for a second that I want to be alone. Come with me, Selene. Just the three of us. For as long as it takes."

Aris stared at Selene, afraid his heart was thundering so violently it was shaking him, so deafeningly she couldn't hear him over its racket.

She looked as if she *hadn't* heard him. Or as if she'd suddenly stopped understanding him.

Or was it only that she thought he'd lost his mind to propose what he had?

And he had. The harsh intellect and uncompromising logic that had governed his life were no more. He was driven by impulse, possessed by desire, tossed about by need without a hint of calculation or premeditation. Nothing was left inside him but one imperative necessity—to be with her and Alex.

He'd been going after them with more single-mindedness than the focus that had seen him to the top. And he'd come to realize both he and she had been wrong about him. He wasn't unfeeling. Where it came to them, he was anything but.

He'd always thought it safer, more efficient, to keep his dealings with others on a practical, cerebral level. He'd never let his family close, never developed the ability to communicate with them, had served them in easily and unequivocally quantifiable ways. His brothers and sisters had their own lives, and he'd never felt they were missing anything by him keeping his distance.

But Selene and Alex were another matter.

Selene and Alex were *his*.

The possessiveness he felt toward both, the overriding emotions, were new, overpowering. All encompassing.

But he couldn't just *say* these feelings existed. He was a man of action. Most important, he had to make sure *he* was capable of handling all that. Having a family of his own was such an enormous concept, it terrified him. At the same time, he couldn't breathe with wanting it. Wanting it all with her. With both of them.

So he'd plunged into the deep end of the frightening, exhilarating unknown territories of being a suitor and one half of a parent duet. He couldn't believe the sheer unbridled…joy just being around them brought, the emptiness he suffered when he had to leave. The anxiety that this might not be for real, for always.

That dread had been increasing by the moment as the world kept intruding when it was all still so new, so fragile and untested. He was terrified of messing up. He couldn't risk letting the world tear them apart before they had something solid that would weather whatever it would throw at them.

Her reaction now compounded his fear. She'd misunderstood him too readily, had agreed to let it end too easily.

Did that mean she hadn't been there with him since they'd started on this journey? Or was it that she simply had no faith in him at all, believed he'd fail her, and Alex, sooner or later, had even been waiting for him to do so?

Was that why she'd found it so easy to believe he already had, and so soon, as to be so pragmatic about accepting his failure, so unaffected by it?

A red-hot lance of disappointment drove through his vitals. But he couldn't even blame her. He wasn't about to wipe away his lifelong track record on the strength of two perfect days and the odd stolen hour over two more weeks.

This made it more imperative that he get the chance to prove to her—and to himself—that he had staying power, that he could be what he longed to be, what they needed him to be.

That chance was all about where and when. Away from the world, now, and for as long as it took.

He repeated his request, urgency bursting in his heart. "Come to Crete with me, Selene. A few weeks in the sun, to forget the demands of the world and concentrate on us, on Alex. I haven't had a vacation in over twenty-five years. I'm sure you haven't had one in at least ten. We owe ourselves and each other time away from everything. Where better than on the golden shores of my homeland?"

Her midnight-sky eyes grew enormous, stormy with an amalgam of tempestuous emotions that buffeted him in turn.

He groaned his plea. "Please, *kala mou*. Say yes."

Yes.

That seemed to be the only word Selene could say to Aris anymore.

She'd said it to his irresistible invitation less than twenty-four hours ago.

She'd set things up with Kassandra, told her brothers she was leaving with her for a much-needed vacation as Kassandra went on a fashion tour through Europe. She told them she'd contact them periodically to let them know that she and Alex were all right.

And here she was, already halfway across the world to where he'd whisked her aboard his private jet. Her and her entourage.

Though he'd assured her that his maternal aunt and her family lived on his estate and they'd have plenty of experienced babysitters to attend Alex when needed, she'd wanted to bring Eleni. He'd told her to invite Eleni's family if she hesitated to leave them behind. It was Selene who'd been hesitant to bring more people, wanting their time together to be as private as possible. But he'd assured her his estate was arranged in such a way that they'd have total privacy even if a hundred people were around. So she'd ended up bringing Eleni and her husband, daughter, son-in-law and grandchildren, the older generation seemingly beside themselves for a chance to go back to the "motherland," and the rest excited to be treated to such an unexpected luxury vacation.

After they'd arrived in Heraklion's airport, Crete's capital, Aris himself had flown them to his estate by the sea in an even more impressive state-of-the-art helicopter. They'd landed half a mile from his mansion, and two limos had been waiting to drive them there.

True to his promise, the limo taking the others headed to buildings nestled among olive groves in a layout that made the estate look like a compound with the main building totally inaccessible from any of the satellite ones, leaving her and Alex to arrive at his house in total privacy.

They came to a stop before the three-story edifice built on the highest point of the land, which then rolled gently to the seashore. The house was ensconced within an explosion of dense thickets of palm trees, pines and cypresses. Beyond their lush cordon lay the most exquisite and seemingly endless landscaped, yet deceptively natural-looking, grounds. Within their vivid embrace the stone-and-plaster building sparkled with the same pristine pale gold as the beaches that spread from its verdant perimeters to the Sea of Crete's waters, the most intense azures and emeralds she'd ever seen.

Selene trembled at the intensity of the stimuli that flooded her, the sensory pleasures cocooning her. From Aris's nearness, to the breathtaking beauty that encompassed them, to the air that enveloped them in its balmy caress. After the nip of cold in NYC's April, the Greek climate embodied spring with its warmth and dryness calibrated to perfect comfort, the air breathing a freshness and purity she could only believe had remained unchanged since the time of the ancient Greeks.

Aris led her up thirty-foot-wide stone steps to a Corinthian-columned portico out of the folds of time. She could now estimate that this place covered around seven thousand square feet and was nestled among at least fifty acres of land with a mile-long beachfront. But it wasn't the size that impacted her, aroused her awe.

She'd lived most of her life in a stately Colonial mansion almost as large, had moved in the circles of those who lived in prodigious homes. But this place was something far more.

With its architecture drawing abundantly yet subtly on ancient Greek themes, Selene felt it siphoning away the strains of the hectic modern life they'd left behind just hours ago. She felt as if it were beckoning them to embrace the tranquility of ancient ways of life. It felt new yet reflected a centuries-old style, was faithful to a millennia-deep culture, catapulting her back to the time of her ancestors. It tugged at her on an elemental level, at the heritage mixed with her blood, but which she'd known only from secondhand accounts, understood only on an intellectual level.

Now, as she walked inside with Aris hugging both her and Alex into the warmth and protection of his body and solicitude, she felt for the first time what it meant to come home.

She sighed with pleasure as the same monumental design greeted her through an interior dominated by unobstructed spaces. There was no pretentiousness, no complex ornamentation or cluttered furniture that served only to flaunt the owner's wealth and questionable taste. And she had no doubt the perfection was all an embodiment of Aris's taste, his eye for the workable, the best.

The expansive entrance gave way to an invitingly simple and sprawling living area draped in utility, comfort and soothing sand tones, with a grand stone-clad fireplace connecting the interior and exterior in spatial and visual terms. The two-story ceiling made her feel she could fly if she wanted to, the flood of golden light pouring from the floor-to-ceiling window imbuing her with such serenity and a sense of freedom and providing an unrestrained view of a stunning internal garden and swimming pool.

A robust, sun-weathered and very good-looking couple in their early sixties entered the house behind them. Selene guessed they must be Aris's aunt Olympia and her husband, Christos. They advanced toward her and Aris with what Selene judged to be more than a little confusion, which deepened when they saw her and Alex and noted Aris containing them within his embrace as if he was afraid they'd evaporate if he loosened his hold.

"Aristedes, you're really here!" the woman exclaimed in Greek, sparing him a glance and pushing back a lock of still mostly dark hair before fastening her gaze on Alex and Selene with utmost curiosity—and in Selene's opinion, not much hope that they might really be who they appeared to be to Aris.

"I bet you thought I wouldn't come...as usual." Aris spoke in Greek, too, making Selene's eyes jerk up to him.

She constantly forgot he was Greek, fully, unlike her. He'd never acquired an American citizenship. But his perfect English, one of the many languages he spoke fluently, did bear the stamp of an accent that she'd found deepened when he was tired. And only served to make every word out of his mouth more unbearably sexy.

Aris guided her and Alex to meet the couple halfway, bent and kissed the woman's cheek before doing the same with the man.

He turned to Selene with such indulgence. "*Kala mou,* please meet *Thia* Olympia and *Thios* Christos." He turned his eyes to the others. "Please welcome Selene Louvardis and our son, Alexandros. I hope you'll help me make their stay here unforgettable."

Her heart quivered.

They were his aunt and uncle. Alex was his son.

She was just herself.

But what else was she? What would he call her? Fleeting ex-lover? Accidental mother-of-his-son? Test-in-progress?

At the mention of his full name, Alex had squeaked out an acknowledgment. Now he pulled at his father's shirt, demanding his attention, to be included. Aris complied at once, bestowed one of those kisses that made Selene feel he was imbuing Alex with his very essence, before he whispered in his ear, and leaned forward, bringing him closer to his aunt.

The older woman's mouth became a circle as her hands rose up, trembling, to receive Alex, who was now willing to be held by whomever at a murmur from his father.

He filled Olympia's embrace with an excited squeal

and her flabbergasted eyes surged with moisture. "Oh, Aristedes, oh, my dearest, at last. Your son!"

Alex looked up at Aris, demanding his praise for doing what he'd told him to do, and so successfully.

Aris delivered it, in that wordless code he'd developed with Alex as he caressed his cheek.

Selene almost whimpered at the intensity and purity of emotions that emanated from his eyes, from his every pore.

And that was before he raggedly said, "Yes, at last."

Over the next few days, they settled in.

Aris gave her and Alex one of the mansion's eight suites, which were almost as big as her condo, and took the one opposite them across a vast hall. She even had her own private staircase to the lower floor, via which Eleni came to babysit Alex.

With Aris there every second that Alex was awake, Eleni took over only when Alex napped. Which he did for longer than usual, expending so much extra energy with the excitement of being with his father all day in what he clearly recognized as a different and magical place.

And when he napped, it was Selene's time alone with Aris.

It was another such time now, on a secluded part of the bay.

They strolled hand in hand in contented silence on the powdered gold sand, letting the surrounding beauty seep through them, and the tranquil rush of the bay's jeweled waters set the tempo of their strides.

She kept stealing hungry glances at Aris. Each time she found him looking at her with an intensity that shuddered through her. Sometimes she shot him a tremulous smile. Sometimes she laughed. Sometimes she whooped, disentangled herself from his hold, sprinted to meet and chase the advance and lure of the gently foaming waves.

And who could blame her? She'd left an on-edge city and life to find herself catapulted here, to a place that put paradise to shame, served and catered to by a god of delights and temptation.

After frolicking like she hadn't done since she was ten, she threw herself onto the warm, cushioning sand, spread her arms as if she'd embrace the cirrus-painted blue dome of the sky and sighed. "And to think I always thought you didn't have a home."

Aris came down beside her, leaned on his elbow and poured his inscrutable silver gaze over her boneless figure. "I don't."

That made her prop herself up on her elbows, look dazedly around, then cautiously back at him. "What about... all this?"

He shrugged a powerful shoulder, cast his steely gaze across the endlessness of the sea. "It's not exactly a home. Not in the sense that I ever intended to live in it."

"Then why did you buy it?"

His eyes moved to hers, translucent like sparkling diamonds yet unfathomable as sealed wells. "Actually I built it."

"Why, if you never intended to live here?"

He shrugged again. "I thought I'd build something for my siblings, in case they ever wanted to come back to live in their homeland. So far they haven't used the place for more than brief vacations."

So he hadn't built this place for himself. Or for a future family, something he'd thought he'd never have. Could someone like him change, embrace ties that he'd lived his life rejecting?

But there must be a reason that he'd built this place *here*.

She tried to find it. "Where you born close by?"

"Actually, I chose this spot because, when I was a boy, this was as far away as possible from where I was born."

So that was his reason. An emotional one. It pained her that it was negative, but it meant he didn't operate solely by cerebral coldness and practical responsibility, had impulses like other human beings.

He cast his gaze wide again, yet seemed to focus internally. "Crete, in this area, is only twelve miles wide. My home was on the other side of the island, overlooking the Libyan Sea. I used to cross the island on foot to go to Agios Nikolaos, a tourist town and port east of Heraklion, where I got my first job on the docks. I began to explore the uninhabited areas, until I came across this bay. I would come here to be alone, run up and down the hill the house is now built on for hours before sitting down to eat, if I had any food with me, looking out to sea as the sun set and the stars or moon dawned. From the time I was ten until I was fifteen, I slept under their canopy more than I did at home. When I made my first million, I bought the land. A few years back I finished building the estate."

So much information, transmitting such heartache and loneliness and hardship, delivered with such conciseness and neutrality. She was dying to learn the specifics of the issues and milestones that had forged him into the man of steel everyone feared, who had no place in his life for anything but takeovers and acquisitions. The man who had acquired a monopoly on her thoughts and desires and was taking over her priorities and future plans.

"Why didn't you ever become an American citizen?"

He exhaled, still not looking at her. "I saw no reason to."

"Your siblings are all Americans now."

Still looking at the horizon as if he could unravel it, he

nodded. "I brought them to America when they were young, and they never wanted to be anywhere else. I wanted to be wherever my work was, to owe no allegiance to one place, with nothing to hold me back and no one to consider in any of my actions or the risks I take. Until the past few weeks, I never wanted anything else."

Then he said no more.

Her heart buzzed inside her chest. With poignancy. With the unbearable crowding of questions. What had he run away from as a boy? Where was his family during those times he'd stayed away from home for nights on end, exposed to the elements, young, vulnerable, alone? Most important, how, just *how,* had he become the man he was today, with evidently everything against him to begin with?

But he'd told her a lot so far of his own accord. And she would wait for answers until he gifted her with more of his truth.

Until then she'd be thankful for what he'd revealed to her. She wouldn't be greedy.

Suddenly he gathered her against his steadily beating heart, reenacted with her what he'd just told her he'd done endless times in his youth—watched the sun melt into the sea, leaving star-studded darkness to rush in to fill the dominion it had rescinded.

And she realized. Not being greedy—when he kept giving her such maddening glimpses of who he was and where he'd come from, far more than she'd ever thought there was to him or for her to have of him—would be the hardest thing she'd yet endeavored.

She had a feeling she'd fail.

Selene looked at the magnificent sight before her and expelled the turmoil vibrating through her on a ragged breath.

Aris, stripped down to the waist, his godlike body now gleaming deep bronze, his muscles flexing in sonnets of power and grace, his hair trapping the sun rays in the palette of its hues. And if that wasn't enough, he was leading an equally, achingly beautiful, perfectly tanned and shrieking-in-delight Alex through his first assisted footsteps on the sand.

She closed her eyes, unable to bear the heart-bursting poignancy. It had been two weeks, and she'd long gotten addicted to Aris. To the sight of him, to his presence, his company. She was becoming dependent on having him transform her and Alex's duo into a trio.

The more he opened up to her, the more he proved that he wasn't just the man she respected as a businessman and lusted after as a lover but the man she could love. *Did* love. With everything in her.

And it was making her insane.

For what if he wanted his son, but not her, too?

She had very good reason to think that might be the case.

She no longer doubted that the bond Aris had formed with Alex was profound and vital, unbreakable and forever. But he hadn't tried to make love to her again. Maybe he no longer wanted *her*. Maybe he had never wanted her. They had come together under extremely stressful conditions, after all.

So what if he was doing whatever it took to prove to her that they could share Alex, without having anything else between them? He *was* an incomparable businessman, and this might all be his comprehensive plan to acquire the son she now knew he wanted with all the single-minded fierceness he was capable of.

She had to know for sure. Or she *would* go insane.

Hours later, after they put Alex to bed, he took her hand

with one of those soul-melting smiles, led her to the kitchen to begin their nightly ritual of preparing their creative dinners.

He was laying out vegetables on the worktop, the spring onions, mushrooms and bell peppers they'd picked from his garden, when she reached critical mass.

She blurted out, "You can give Alex your name."

He snapped up his head as if she'd shot him.

He stared at her, his eyes widening, his face slackening, shock visibly shaking him, rocking him on his feet.

Just as she was about to scream for him to say something, his eyes shimmered and he choked, "*Theos,* Selene…you mean it?"

She nodded, her own throat clogging with tears. Of delight for his obvious agonizing joy. Of dreadful anticipation.

"You want Alex to be Alexandros Sarantos?" His voice shook.

She could only nod again. If she had functioning vocal chords left, she would have begged him to put her out of her misery.

Do you want me *to be Selene* Sarantos, *too?*

An urgent rap on the door made them both jerk with the force of the intrusion.

Tearing his turbulent gaze from hers, he swung around and rushed to the door. It was Olympia. Though Selene spoke Greek well, she understood only the highlights of Olympia's outburst. Christos had fallen off a ladder and injured himself.

Aris sent his aunt back to Christos before rushing to Selene.

He towered over her, looming bigger as delight mixed with worry emanated from his every pore. Then he hugged her off the ground.

Next second, he turned and rushed away.

Within fifteen minutes, she heard the chopper taking off.

Shortly thereafter, he called. She picked up immediately, heard his voice raised above the chopper's din. "Christos broke his shoulder. I'm flying him to a hospital in Heraklion."

She winced. She hated to think of the lively Christos in pain, incapacitated. "I hope it isn't too bad. Take care, please. And give him my best wishes."

"I will. Selene…" He paused. Her heartbeats did, too. He finally exhaled. "When you said you'll let me give Alex my name, you meant only that?" She closed her eyes, her heart rattling, unable to bear anticipating his next words. "To give him my name but not be his father, fully? I know it's been only a month since this all started, but… *Theos,* Selene! Do you still suspect the depth of my commitment? You think I'll sooner or later consider huge bank deposits and assets in his name a substitute for love and being there for him as I always did? Are you still afraid I'll eventually disappear from his life?"

"No!" She didn't doubt his commitment. Not to Alex. *But what do I mean to you?* She restrained the outburst with a force that shook her. "I'm now sure you won't be the absentee father I feared you would be. I believe you'll be the very opposite."

His ragged exhalation shuddered through her.

When next he spoke, he sounded high with relief and delight. "Thank you, Selene. You will never regret this decision."

A cry rang out. For moments she thought it had come from her.

His voice receded on a growl. "*Theos,* don't move!" He

spoke to her this time. "I have to hang up now. Thank you again, *kala mou*."

The line went dead.

As dead as the rock that suddenly filled her chest.

He hadn't brought up anything between *them*.

He wanted only Alex.

Eight

Aris stayed away all of the next day, making sure his aunt and her husband had the very best care.

It was seven in the morning, after another night in hell, when she heard the front door open. She felt her heart plummet with every heavy footstep taking him to her.

She would tell him now. That she wanted to go home.

Their test had been concluded. And he'd passed it. He would be Alex's father. It was time to find out how he planned to work that out once they went back to the real world. No need for them to remain here.

He came into the kitchen. He looked grim and haggard—and the zenith of male beauty. Her breath sheared through her lungs as he approached her, his gaze denuding in intensity.

"Is—is Christos okay?"

"He'll be fine. I flew in the best orthopedic surgeon and his team from Athens." A pause. His gaze bored into her, as if he could extract every bit of information out of her gray matter. "When you said you'll let me be Alex's father, was that it? You don't want me as your husband?"

Her heart staggered inside her. Was he asking, to be clear? Or was he offering? And if he was, was it for the right reason?

For the first time in his life, Aris would let something sway him, rule him. Alex's best interests would make him do *anything*. She owed him the freedom of an unpressured choice. And herself the truth of his feelings, whatever they were.

This was the hardest, scariest thing she ever had to do. Then she did it, breathed, "We don't come attached in one deal, Aris. Being Alex's father has nothing to do with being my husband."

His eyebrows dipped lower, deepening his grimness. "Being his father *and* your husband was always the deal."

Her every cell began to churn with hope. But she had to be beyond certain. "Then your negotiating skills are fraying, because that certainly didn't seem to be what you're offering."

His jaw muscles bunched. "What are you talking about? I asked you to marry me that very first day."

She nodded, still scared that she was reading what she was dying to see in his eyes. "Yeah—for Alex. That's no reason to get married. I told you back then, when I refused your rash and offhand marriage proposal…"

His eyes flared. "You mean, when *you* laughed *my* head off."

That rankled, huh? Joy began to bubble inside her, came out as unstoppable goading. "*After* which you promptly followed up with a very detailed withdrawal and admission that you weren't husband material, followed by a very relieved dropping of the subject."

He shook his head as if he couldn't believe what he was hearing. "What do you think the last four weeks were about? All this talk about testing me, finding out what I can be for *both* of you?"

Her body hummed in anticipation of setting off in fireworks of jubilation. "Being on good terms with the mother of your son?"

He barked an incredulous laugh. "Good terms? And here I thought we were on the *best* of terms."

"I don't think so."

His gaze wavered. "You don't?"

She was pushing too hard. But she had to hear him say the words. "We're not on *those* kind of terms—the kind that lead to being husband and wife. Though four weeks ago I would have never thought it possible, you *do* make a great best friend. So don't think you have to offer me marriage for Alex's sake. We can go on like we have been. Great friends, and great parents to Alex."

He glowered down at her for an endless moment.

Just when she thought he'd tell her she was an insecure fool, then snatch her into his arms and devour her as proof that he'd never settle for anything like that, for less than all of her, that he wanted and had always wanted her, for herself, he turned on his heel.

She stared at his receding back.

He was *leaving?* B-but…he couldn't be!

She jerked as the front door slammed after him.

She still waited, unable to believe he wouldn't come back.

He didn't.

Was it possible that her worst fears hadn't been paranoia but the truth?

She didn't know how long she'd stood there, numb, trembling.

She finally moved, dragged herself up to Alex's room.

She couldn't let pain take her over. For his sake. She had to remain on the best possible terms with Aris. It was his right to be part of his son's life without being with her. His right to love his son, without loving her.

Alex was stirring. She picked him up, hugged him, tears slithering down her cheeks to wet his silky hair.

She was happy. For him. He'd now have a father who loved him for life, not just a mother. As for her, she had to regain the self she'd been before she lost her heart to Aris, a man who had no use for it. She had no illusions that she'd reclaim it, or find happiness. All she could hope for was finding refuge from the agony, maybe a measure of peace.

Hours later, she'd packed and was playing with Alex while inwardly reciting what she'd tell Aris to end this amicably, set up their future interaction, when an urgent knock rapped on the front door.

She dragged herself to open it. It was Taki, Aris's driver.

The stocky, swarthy man blurted out, "*Kyrios* Sarantos wants you to come with me at once, *Kyria* Louvardis."

Alarm detonated inside her. "Is he all right?"

The man looked at her as if she'd said something ludicrous. "He's *waiting* for you."

Dazedly, she turned to Eleni, who'd already taken her place by Alex. Eleni only beamed at her, said to take her time.

Resigned that she'd know what this was about only when she saw Aris, she stumbled to his limo. For the next twenty minutes, she gazed at the Mediterranean, sun-drenched beauty as the smooth, black asphalt road took them deep through the surrounding vegetation-covered hills before undulating back to the emerald shore.

Finally, Taki came to a stop beside Aris's Porsche. Taki rushed to hand her out of the car. But he and everything else evaporated from her awareness like a drop of water on a hot tin roof.

All she could register was the scene before her.

A hundred feet away, at the end of a deep red carpet, spread with gold dust and white rose petals, lined by flaming torches and a conflagration of lilies, stood a huge white tent flapping gently in the late-afternoon breeze, just feet from the water.

At the end of the path of fire and flowers, there he was. Aris, in white shirt and pants that hugged every slope and bulge of his perfection and offset his glowing tan. The layered waves of the sun-kissed hair that he hadn't cut since he'd come back into her life flowed around his leonine head and brushed his formidable shoulders, as if beckoning her closer.

Not that she needed enticement. She had to get close, had to see in his eyes the reflection of this gift a woman could live her life dreaming of and never attain a fraction of. If this was what he felt he should do, or what he truly felt.

She teetered toward him on legs powered by his lure, her enthrallment. Her own hair seemed to come alive in the breeze. She was struggling with its intrusion when she stopped a foot from him, the exact second he went down.

She gasped, almost fell over him.

He'd—he was—Aris was…*kneeling* before her.

Everything inside her seized.

She'd never—*never*—thought he, Aristedes Sarantos, would put himself in such a position of supplication, no matter what.

But he was. Then he was doing more.

He extended a velvet box the color of the sea at its deepest. He opened it and she gasped again.

A sapphire, the most perfect stone she'd ever seen, the exact color of her eyes, caught the deepening gold of the sun rays and the flickering flames and radiated them back at her in a rainbow of hypnosis.

She tore her eyes from the jewel to his own twin diamonds, found them ablaze with what rivaled the heat of both flames and sun.

And he groaned, "*Will* you marry me, *agape mou?*"

Aris looked up at Selene, his heart barely pumping any blood, as if it was holding its breath like he was.

The stunned look in her eyes didn't boost his equilibrium. When no ecstatic "yes" trembled on her lips, a terrible thought detonated inside him.

What if she hadn't been telling him that his earlier efforts to make her his had been lamentable, but that she didn't want to *be* his? That she was content to share Alex with him, but nothing more? Had his hands-off policy only served to make her realize she didn't want him after all?

Or maybe he was doing *this* all wrong. Maybe he looked ridiculous to her, the cerebral, cynical lawyer, seeing him, the last person on earth she could imagine being sentimental, down on one knee, calling her his love, and looking up at her as if he'd suffocate if she didn't give him a favorable answer.

He retracted the hand offering the ring she hadn't reached for, rose slowly to his feet, decided to hope he was guilty of option two, the lesser evil by far here. "I botched up my first proposal. Am I doing it all wrong again?"

The shock seizing her face fractured. Her features trembled for a second then melted and a melodious sound burst from the lush lips he'd been suffering agonies not tasting.

She was laughing.

At him. At his offer. Again.

His shoulders slumped. What had he expected? That he'd exit a life of emotional exile and suddenly develop the complex skills needed to communicate his newfound emotions?

He looked down at the ring in the box dangling from his nerveless hand, exhaled. "It all seemed so right to me...in theory."

Her laughter ended abruptly. He raised his eyes to hers, again felt the overwhelming sense of rightness, of everything about her slotting into all the empty places inside him, filling them, completing him. How could he live if he didn't complete her?

He groaned his insecurity, something he'd only ever incurred on her account. "Will you overlook this? I'm suffering from a lifetime of emotional disuse. I want to please you, to honor you, to show you how much I want you to be mine, but I seem unable to get it right...."

Her hand stopped his before he stuffed the box into his pocket. "I can't begin to think how you could have gotten it *more* right." His gaze sharpened on her. Her eyes were growing heavy lidded, her lips dewy and flushed, as if he'd already kissed her senseless as he was burning to. "My wildest fantasies wouldn't have come up with—" she flung her hands wide, before converging them on him in a sweep as elegant as a ballet dancer's "—*this*."

He shuddered at the things he didn't dare interpret in her eyes, at the jolt of hope. And confusion. "Then...*why?*"

"Why did I laugh this time? Because you, the all-knowing Aristedes Sarantos, seem to suffer the same misapprehensions I was suffering from...till a moment ago."

"What misapprehensions?" he rasped.

A cast of vulnerability, of relived hurt and despair entered her eyes, made him want to tear down the whole world so that he'd never see anything like that in her eyes again.

She lowered her eyes, took that mutilating expression away. "When you didn't try to make love to me again, I thought you didn't want me as much as you thought you did."

That had been her fear?

"You were right." That brought her eyes snapping up to his, that ready pain flooding them again. So she, too, felt incomplete without him, so much so that fearing he didn't feel the same plunged her into despair. He'd pay his very life for her to never feel that way again. And he pledged, "I want you far more than I knew I was capable of. My desire for you defines me now. It is who I am—the man who wants you."

Her heavenly eyes flickered with an alternation of surging delight and receding dejection as she gave him back his moments-ago uncertainty. "Then…why?"

"Fool that I am, I was trying to rewind and do things in the right order. I feared sexual intimacy would overwhelm us, that other pleasures we could find together would go undiscovered. So I held back, being only a 'great friend' to you. At the price of pieces of my sanity."

"And mine."

Her confession was searing in its truth, its totality.

She wanted him. As much as he wanted her.

It was almost inconceivable.

How could he possibly deserve it?

But she did. She *did*. And he'd live his life from now on to deserve every spark of desire she bestowed on him, to prove to her she'd done the right thing, the best thing for her, wanting him.

This time when he fell to his knees before her, it was

with the enervation of relief. He extended his hand up with the ring to her again. "Will you have mercy on me, save what's left of mine?"

Her face quaked with a joy so fierce, he almost wept seeing it. Then she extended a trembling hand back to him.

She wanted him to put his ring on her finger, do the running. And he would, for the rest of his life, if only she'd always let him catch her.

His hand shook as he slipped the ring on her finger before smothering her in his passion and gratitude. "And to think you mistook my restraint for lack of interest, when I thought I was building up anticipation."

She moaned a laugh. "You did. How you did. You almost kill me with how well you do everything. Will *you* have mercy on me now?"

Blind, out of his mind with hunger and thankfulness and the need to claim her, conquer her, surrender to her, he surged to his feet, filled his arms with her, his moon goddess, magic-and-night-and-life made woman. *His* woman. The woman he'd been made for.

"You're saying yes, Selene?" he groaned against her lips in between wrenching kisses. "Yes to me, to a lifetime with me?" Her nod was frantic, her lips as rapacious, giving him back his frenzy. "Yes to anything I want to do to you now and from now on?"

This time when she nodded, her breath made a catching sound deep in her chest, feminine greed and surrender made audible.

His body jerked with a clap of thundering arousal as his hardness turned from rock to steel. He wanted her to make this sound again, and again, to make her scream and sob in a delirium of pleasure as he ravaged her, devoured her, dissolved inside her.

He slammed her harder against him, lost another notch of control as she arched into him, offering him her all. He looked down at her, peach tingeing her newly acquired tan, her pupils engulfing the twilight skies of her irises, turning them to pitch darkness. A darkness that siphoned his sanity, his separateness. He wanted to lose himself in her, never resurface, never be apart from her flesh and essence again.

"Say you're mine, Selene."

"I'm yours…yours, Aris."

This. What he hadn't known he'd been living for. His greatest triumph. The only one worth anything. Worth it all.

"Yes, Selene. Mine to worship and pleasure." He took her from gravity, clamped the lips trembling agreement and incitement beneath his, thrust deep into the fount of her taste. He groaned in the sweetness she surrendered with such mind-destroying eagerness, to himself, to her, to the fates that had placed her, a gift he'd never thought he deserved let alone would find, in his path. "Keep saying you're mine, Selene, make me believe it."

She kept saying it as he swept her into the tent he hadn't dared visualize would witness anything this sublime.

He fast-forwarded to the nine-by-nine bed he'd placed in the middle, spread with silk sheets the color of her eyes. He arranged her in its center and she unfurled around him like a wildflower.

He pulled back from her frantic grasp, the need to feast on her hammering at him. He dragged down her sky-blue dress, exposing her to the rhythm of his promises of possession, of her pleas to take all of her. He replaced the supple cloth's cover with his lips, tongue and teeth, coating her velvet firmness in suckles and nips. Her moans guided him where to skim and tantalize, where to linger and torment, where to draw harder and devour, their heightening frenzy as they transformed to keens then labored gasps a testament to his rising skill in pleasuring her.

The accumulation of need was reaching critical levels. But he couldn't let their first intimacy in so long, what would seal their lifelong pact, begin a lifetime of escalating pleasures, be anything less than perfect bliss for her. His pleasure, as it had when he'd first claimed her, would always stem from hers.

He had mercy on her, on himself, slid the dress all the way off, lingering on a long groan as he took her panties with it, freeing one silky leg after the other from the confines.

Then he pulled back. Looked down on his goddess.

He'd seen all of her before, before Alex, had seen her in the torture devices that were her one-piece swimsuits since. He'd thought he'd known the extent of the wonder of her.

He'd thought wrong. For here she was. Beyond his memories and observations. Ripe, strong, tailored to his every fastidious taste. This was *her*. His woman. And she was dying for him as he was for her, quaking with the force of her need.

"You're far more than I remember." He heard the awe in his voice, felt his heart shake at the pride and pleasure and lingering vulnerability in her eyes. "And how I remembered. Incredible, *agape mou,* mind-blowing."

She held out her arms in demand, in supplication, and he yanked her to him, bending her across one arm. She splashed her supple arms and ebony waterfall over his flesh in abandon, arched in an erotic offering he'd sacrifice anything for.

"*Ne,* Selene, *ne,* every inch of you, give it to me, beg for it all with me, I beg you."

She complied, at once, her voice fracturing with passion.

"Take all of me, do everything to me, let me have all of you."

"You won't hold anything back, Selene. Never again. You'll always let me do everything to you, with you, for you."

She writhed her consent to his commands, opened wide for the litanies of passion he poured into her lips. Then he moved down, suckling her pulse as if he'd take her life force inside himself, mingle it with his own. He kneaded and weighed the perfect orbs of her breasts, turgid in her extreme arousal, pinched the resilience and need of her peach-colored nipples, dialing her arousal higher. Before he fractured with hunger, he swooped down and captured the buds of overpowering femininity in his mouth.

She rewarded each pull with a soft, shuddering shriek, then more as his hands glided over her abdomen, closed over the trim mound beneath.

This. Where he'd merged them, where he'd invaded her, where she'd captured him. Where he'd thrust them both over one edge after another into abysses of abandon and ecstasy. Where she'd received his seed, took his essence, purified it, transformed it into the magic of life. Where she'd given him the other half of his soul and reason for his existence, Alex.

He squeezed his eyes, her flesh. "This is my home, *agape mou*. My only home."

"Aris." Her cry speared him, a molten lance in his soul, a steel shaft in his loins. "Yes, my love, yes…come home inside me."

My love. Hearing that, on her satin voice, like a prayer, an homage, was like a physical blow to his vitals. He'd hoped. Then he'd known. But to hear her say it… *Too much.*

He couldn't be that blessed, could he?

He growled with unbearable stimulation, with humility,

slid two fingers between the satin slickness of her exquisite folds, spreading them, getting high on the scent of her arousal, the evidence of her desire and feminine nectar.

He slipped a careful finger, then two inside her, grunted with another blast of arousal. Soaking for him, but so tight…

"Just come inside me," she choked. "Come home, Aris… *please.*"

"Let me give you pleasure first, prepare you. I won't be gentle in my possession."

She cried out at his sensual threat, opened herself for its execution, rewarding him with a new rush of arousal over his fondling fingers. He heard himself rumbling like a leashed beast as he spread the flowing honey, his thumb finding the knot of flesh that housed her trigger. He'd barely stroked it when her cries of pleasure, of his name, stifled and she came apart in his arms.

He roared with pride as he drew out her release, rode its waves, pumping his fingers inside her clamping flesh, stroking her inside and out, loosening her, suckling her nipples until he felt her flesh rippling around his fingers again, tension reinvading her body. He spread her core, bent, gave her one long lick, the ravenous beast inside him maddened for her taste and scent.

She tried to squeeze her legs, her eyes wet and beseeching. "Aris, please, you now, you…"

"Not yet. Now I need to feed. I've been starving for you, *agape mou.* Nineteen endless months. Let me have my fill."

She nodded mutely, her color dangerous, and spread herself wide for him.

He slid her over the sheets' smoothness and kneeled before her again, open and willing, overpowering him with her submission. Blood was a geyser in his head, his manhood. He gritted his teeth, brought her silky, shaking limbs over his shoulders, filling his aching hands with the firmness of her velvet buttocks.

He nudged her thighs with his face, latching wide-open lips on their flesh. "Watch me worship you, *agape mou*, take your pleasure watching me pleasure you, own your every secret."

She squirmed, hiccuped then nodded, sat up on her elbows, spreading her core's lips against his.

He grunted as lust jackknifed in his system. "Beauty like this should be outlawed." Then he plunged in.

He captured her between sucking lips and massaging teeth, circling her knot, subduing her gently as she thrashed with each corkscrewing lick and insistent pull, bringing her to the edge, listening to the music of her explicit ecstasy. He felt her flood with it, hurtling toward completion. He placed a palm on her heart until he felt it start to miss beats. Then he blew on her quivering, engorged flesh, tongue-lashed her. She shredded her throat with ecstasy, unraveled her body in a chain reaction of convulsions. And looked him in the eye all through.

That was eroticism. That was intimacy and fulfillment.

Everything with her had been that.

Now he would take her, and union with her would reinvent those concepts. He hoped she was ready for him now.

He slid up her sweat-slick body, flattening her to the mattress, soaking up her drugged look, the slackness confessing the depth of her satiation.

He branded her lips, let her taste her pleasure on his, and her hips undulated her urgency against his bursting arousal, gave him what he'd wanted earlier. The hitching, broken-from-too-much-need sounds echoing in her depths.

It had been that way during those two days of magic that had resulted in the miracle of Alex. She'd been unable to get enough of him, as he hadn't of her.

She tore at his shirt, at his pants, her voice dark and husky. "Give me…all of you."

He felt his last tether of sanity snapping and he took her lips in rough, moist kisses, nothing left in him but the driving need to cede all to her, bury himself inside her.

He came over her, impacted her, felt her softness cushioning his hardness. She opened her legs, enveloped him in their embrace.

He obeyed her demand, brought his shaft to her entrance, slid partway into her nectar, stimulating her more, bathing himself, struggling not to ram inside her, to ride her with all his power.

She whimpered, arched to bring him closer, and he surrendered, flexed his hips, plunged into her heat.

He went blind with the blast of pleasure.

When his sight returned, he saw her arched off the bed, sensations slashing across her face, pain among the feverish ingredients. The velvet vise enveloping him, even now, was almost too tight. Their fit was still almost impossible, and the only one that would ever be right. Yet, he'd hurt her….

"Forgive me," he panted. "I should have been more gentle."

Her legs yanked him tighter against her, forcing him to stroke deeper into her body, tearing a hot sharp sound from her depths. "You *promised* you wouldn't be."

He stroked inside her, still hesitating when her face contorted with that maddening amalgam of ecstasy and agony.

"Sarantos, don't you dare hold back on me now."

It was that *Sarantos*. That lash of overpowering challenge.

He thrust inside her, hard, impaled her to her womb.

"Yes." At her welcoming cry, he thrust harder, then harder. Her body quaked with the force of his plunges, her cries sharpened with each, incoherent, yet eloquent with her need for his ferociousness. She never took her gaze away from his, let him see every sensation ripping through her. She seemed to glow with her rising pleasure, every inch of her a work of divine art the master poets and artists of ancient Greece would have failed to depict.

Her fingers bunched in his hair, bringing his lips down to drown them both in the shoreless reaches of abandon, as he rode her to the rhythm of a sea that seemed to have caught their frenzy. With the roaring building of a wave, he withdrew from her clenching depths, only to ram all the way back inside her with its crash. And she shattered around him.

The feel and sight of her ecstasy made him surge to her womb, release his seed there, images of another miracle, a tiny replica of her this time, sending him almost berserk with its poignancy.

At the first splash of his essence against her intimate flesh, her convulsions intensified, tearing his orgasm from depths even she hadn't plumbed before. He discovered new depths inside her, too, jetted his agonizing release in endless surges, filling her, his roars harmonizing with her stifled shrieks and with the rumbles of a suddenly tempestuous sea.

He felt her melt beneath him, jerking with the aftershocks jolting through them both. He throbbed inside her, hard and maddened for more. But he had to give her respite.

He twisted, brought her draping over him. She lay inert,

humming a wonderful sound, a score of bliss. He thought she slept for minutes. He studied her nuances, counted her every calming breath, and knew he'd never known contentment till now.

He was almost sorry when she stirred. He could have watched her forever. Next second, his heart was hurtling with delight that she had. She wobbled up, sending the sensual feast of her hair brushing over his chest and his heartbeats scattering all over the cloth floor of the tent.

She gave him a smile that made him feel he could fly. And that was before she slid over him, dipped her head to his pulse and drew coherence from his body with soul-stealing suckles.

Then she tore his sanity away irrevocably when she whispered, "Do you know how it feels to have you inside me? I was empty without you. Never leave me empty again, my love."

His own confession shook out of him. "Hunger for you consumed me, too. Take me inside you always, *agape mou*. Never let me go."

"Yes…Aris, never again. Let me have you now." He reared back to obey her. She stopped him. "*I* want *all* of you this time."

He stared at her. But he thought he'd given her all of him.

She struggled up on her elbows, a goddess of sensual abandon and delirious nights, her smile a lethal mind-altering narcotic. "I want every inch of what's mine. You *are* mine to do with as I please, too, aren't you?"

And he understood. His shirt was ripped open, his pants undone only to free his arousal. Before he took her again, she wanted to take him, own him as he'd owned her.

He rose to expose himself fully to her ownership, make

her an offering of his body and potency, all the while pledging, "Yours, Selene. Yours, *agape mou,* never anyone else's."

Selene lay back, struck mute, dizzy with the aftershocks of what Aris had done to her, yet ready for more. For anything.

And there he was, Aris, stripping for her, piling arousal on arousal. The sudden wildness of the sea and wind outside plunged them into a primal realm. The light flickering from the brass lamps and the tent's flapping opening drenched the flower-filled interior in a mystical ambiance. It all synergized to echo the vigor of his vibe, the power of his sexuality and the endlessness of his stamina and magnanimity, to offset his physical wonder, worshipping the perfect sculpture, strength and grace of his body.

He came to stand over her and the sunbeams cascading from the tent's seams caught him in their crisscrossed spotlight, illuminating slashes and slopes of dark magic across his beloved face and honed, glistening, dauntingly aroused body.

She could barely believe it. All this was hers?

Before she begged him to reassure her, he bent, groaned in her ear, "Yours, Selene. Own me."

She flung herself at him, buried her face into his ridged abdomen, breathed and tasted him, her itching hands seeking the hot, steel length of him.

He stabbed his fingers into her hair as she opened her lips over the silky crown, lapped the addicting flow of his arousal.

He thrust himself deeper into her possession, growled his pleasure. "Hurry and take your fill of me this way, Selene. I need to take my turn in owning you, filling your needs."

She didn't hurry, took her time, possessed him in every

way she'd been going crazy for. Then, when she thought she'd drained him, he proved her wrong, remained ready to fulfill his promise.

And for the rest of the night, he did. How he did.

Selene spent the next days wondering if this could be real.

But it *was*. Beyond real. Vivid. All encompassing.

Their intimacy escalated, on all fronts. Aris opened up more every day, letting her into his past, his mind, his business. She felt happiness so acute it scared her. The world never let bliss like this continue, always conspired to shatter it.

As if to validate her fear, one afternoon while they lazed around the inside pool, Aris received a phone call.

She was bending to pick up Alex when he answered.

He did so only to fall silent for a long, long moment.

A frisson of foreboding slithered down her spine.

She looked over at him, found him looking at her, his eyes filled with something...terrible.

Next second, his eyes went blank. He looked away, ended the phone call on some curt orders.

But she still *felt* it. Something...dark, mushrooming inside him. Anxiety burst in her chest.

Then it all happened at once.

She started to move toward Aris. She heard the sickening thud. She saw Aris jerk as if he'd been shot. Then the wail exploded.

She looked down, found Alex on his back, screaming his lungs out. At the periphery of her vision, she saw Aris streaking toward them. Her mind streaked, too, making sense of what had happened.

While she'd been preoccupied with Aris's reaction to the phone call, Alex had managed to take off his nonslip sandals. And he'd slipped on a wet patch. That terrible sound had been his head hitting the roughened marble.

The next second, his wails stopped. And he started convulsing.

Nine

During the nightmare that followed, Selene learned the meaning of terror. And of having Aris with her.

When she'd thought she'd always be a single parent, she'd realized that, especially in times of crisis, she would miss the support Alex's father could have provided.

But Aris wasn't just a father to Alex, or a partner for her. As someone who'd created and commanded his own empire, he possessed powers of almost inhuman efficiency, of limitless and levelheaded intervention. He was the best person on earth to deal with whatever life threw at them.

And this was the worst life had dealt her.

As she realized Alex was having a seizure, macabre scenarios attacked her with paralyzing viciousness. Alex could suffer permanent brain damage, could die. They might lose him.

And it was her fault.

But Aris wouldn't let her go to pieces. His soothing

commands and assurances defused her havoc, insisted that accidents happened. Even the unconscious Alex seemed to respond to his father's support, as he told him that he'd never let anything bad happen to him, that he'd take care of everything. And he did.

Within minutes, he had her, Alex and Eleni onboard his helicopter. He arranged everything during the flight. When they landed at the hospital's emergency helipad, an ambulance and a team of doctors were waiting.

Alex's resuscitation and tests were concluded in less than thirty minutes. During which Selene would have fallen apart if not for Aris being there, holding her, murmuring encouragement and imbuing her with his power and stability.

Then Alex was brought out of the emergency room, awake but disoriented. He whimpered at the sight of them, threw himself toward her first, but then he wanted to be in Aris's arms, burrowing deep into his father's power and protection and promptly fell asleep.

Each doctor told his specialty's story. Alex had suffered a concussion but the danger was past and he was expected to bounce back within a day without complications, and at worst a period of fussiness due to possible headaches. The advised forty-eight-hour hospital stay was just for further observation.

Even with their assurances, and with Alex waking up as if nothing had happened, Selene still counted the time until their discharge as the most harrowing of her life.

Then they were back on Aris's estate, and she realized the nightmare hadn't ended.

At first she chalked it up to still being shaken, that she was imagining tension where none existed. Or that Aris's disturbance was, like hers, due to lingering worry about Alex.

But she could no longer believe that. That phone call had borne him terrible news. News he didn't share. This disturbed her as much as anything else. She couldn't bear to think he was suffering alone, that he thought he couldn't come to her with any worries, halve them by letting her bear the burden with him.

But something she couldn't define kept her from asking. Something huge that she felt hanging over them, over their future. And she was scared to look it in the eye, let it be real, let it wreak its devastation on them.

After they put Alex to bed, she reached breaking point.

She couldn't share the rest of their evening rituals then go to bed with him feeling this way.

They were walking away from Alex's nursery when she put her hand on Aris's arm. His gaze jerked to hers. She saw the warmth that suffused his eyes when Alex was around drain to be replaced by something dark and bleak, like ink spreading through pristine waters.

It dissipated as soon as it formed, making her wonder whether she'd seen it. But she had. Even if he was now smiling at her. She knew his every expression down to its last nuance by now. And this smile originated from premeditation and not a little effort. Something was wrong. Something big. Momentous. And that brilliant mind of his was working overtime trying to decide on the least damaging way to deal with it.

But when he pulled her into his side, everything dissipated in the yearning for his nearness, for everything to be all right with him, for their perfect bliss to resume.

As they reached the kitchen, he kissed the top of her head before he spooled her away and headed to the fridge.

As he opened it, he looked over his shoulder. "He's fine." Her gaze clung to his across the distance. He'd read that part of her turmoil right. "And for the last time, it wasn't your fault."

And she heard herself blurt out, "I want to go home."

Aris stilled for what felt like an eternity.

Everything inside her came to a halt, too.

She didn't know where that outburst had come from.

But then, she did. She suddenly felt trapped here, powerless. She felt she'd regain control, of herself at least, on her own turf. She also believed Aris needed to go back to deal with whatever was weighing on his mind, but he wouldn't think of leaving if he thought she wanted to stay.

She watched him with her heart hammering in her throat as he closed the fridge and turned to her in movements loaded with calculated tranquility. He'd ask why, and all her reasons suddenly sounded stupid.

But he didn't ask. With his face an expressionless mask, he only said, "As you wish."

There had never been anything she wished less.

She'd told him so, that she wished their time in Crete could have never ended, that she'd love to return, soon and always.

He'd smiled, assured her they'd return whenever she wished, was as indulgent as ever. But his words and actions contradicted what she sensed from him. He seemed to have shut down inside.

She told herself this would pass. That he was priming himself to deal with whatever problem he clearly had. That once things stabilized, they'd regain their rapport, indulge in the wide-open channels of communication they'd established.

Within twenty-four hours, they were back in the city where she'd lived all her life. And it no longer felt like home. Home was where she'd become Aris's, where they'd become a family.

She was smiling up at him as he held Alex and pushed her condo's door open for her, when her heart stopped.

At the pure aggression in his eyes.

She swung around. Gasped, gaped.

Her three brothers were in her foyer, filling it with their towering bodies and answering hostility.

No. She couldn't handle this now. Her brothers finding out about her and Aris, coming here to…to…

Steel seeped into her bones, replacing the jelly of shock.

What *did* they want, anyway? Who did they think they were, coming here and policing her life?

Before she could preempt them with a few choice rebukes, her middle brother, Lysandros, came forward, his smirk twisting a face she'd heard described as one the progeny of an angel and a demon would have. "Ah, the happy family returns."

Damon gave an impressive snort. "Yeah, very touching."

So they knew. She would have preferred to tell them herself, but this was her life, and Aris was an inseparable and indispensable part of it now. They had to deal with it. Their presence here might turn out to be a blessing in disguise—they could have it out now and get on with their lives.

She tore her gaze away from them, needing to reconnect with Aris, to wordlessly tell him he didn't need to fight them for rights to her and Alex. She and Alex were *his,* but, these were her brothers, and she loved them. With the way he was looking, she wouldn't put it past him to attack them. Knowing her roughhousing brothers, they were probably itching for him to make a move. She wouldn't let them have a testosterone-driven free-for-all and end up maybe injured, and certainly on worse terms than ever.

She was the reason for their current hostilities, and she had to defuse the situation, install the terms of their future relationship. One—hopefully—governed by friendship, and failing that, at least peaceful coexistence.

But Aris didn't meet her eyes. Her mortification morphed to shock as she realized *what* she saw in his expression. He'd been...expecting them.

She looked back to her brothers for an explanation. But they, too, were ignoring her. They closed in on Aris like a pack of wolves on a hyena who had a female and a cub of theirs in his clutches.

At that moment, Alex whimpered.

They all jerked, focused on him. He was looking from the uncles he loved to his even more beloved father with trepidation.

Seeming to feel the unequal odds against his father, to decide they represented danger to him, he declared which side he chose, clung to Aris tighter and buried his face in his chest.

That stopped her brothers in their tracks.

Aris soothed Alex with kisses and murmurs she couldn't hear, before looking behind him at the frozen Eleni, whom Selene had forgotten about, too.

Without a word, Eleni rushed to take Alex from Aris and disappeared deep into the condo with him.

An awkward moment passed, the contrite looks that had come over her brothers for inadvertently upsetting Alex receding. Then they resumed forming their blockade around Aris.

"Did you hear, Sarantos?" Nikolas began, making her realize again how much in common he and Aris had. It made the hostility arcing between them hurt more. These two men should be allies, as Aris had once said of her father. They had so much to offer one another, so much they could share. She hoped, once this was resolved, they would develop the relationship she ached for Aris to have with all her brothers. Nikolas came to a stop a foot away from Aris, looked him up and down like someone who didn't know where to start hurting someone. "I bet you did."

Damon barked another harsh snort. "Look at him. Of course he heard. His watchdogs must have run to him with the news as soon as his strategically disseminated insiders leaked it to them."

What were they talking about? Aris's bad news? She hadn't thought they'd stoop to gloating over a business loss in this intensely personal situation, but she could think of nothing else.

"So how does it feel, Sarantos?" Nikolas inclined his head at the till-now ominously silent Aris. "To be kicked to the curb for once in your charmed life? To have a blot on your perfect conquest record? And not just any blot. This one is going to hurt, the worst you've ever felt. It will be like I told you, the beginning of the end for you."

"You did have us stymied for a while." Lysandros took the baton from his older brother without missing a beat. "But we broke your stalemate. You must be going mad wondering how we did. But now *we're* steering the U.S. Navy contract, and it gives me great pleasure to say this to your face. You're out of the running. We're bringing in the Di Giordanos."

Selene blinked, unable to take in the barrage of unexpected information. Was this true? If it was, then this must be the news that had hit Aris so hard. But how had they done it? There was no way Aris hadn't guarded against something like this. How could they have eliminated him that easily?

Damon's gloating interrupted her confusion. "But you were desperate for this contract, weren't you? You were determined to win it any way you could. So while you put roadblocks in our path, you were making sure you'd get it another way if those failed. So you infiltrated us through our weak link. Selene."

Selene's heart almost fired from her ribs with shock.

They thought…thought…

Before the ghastly accusations could sink, Nikolas took over. "You knew about Alex all along, didn't you? But you only decided to pursue Selene, and be his 'father,' to enter the Louvardis family and make it impossible for us to remain your enemies."

No. The scream detonated. Only inside her.

The horror of what they were suggesting made her mute. This was a serious crime they were accusing him of, far worse than anything their father had recommended they stand together against him for.

How would she take them from such complete demonizing of Aris to the perfect trust she now had in him?

Lysandros was going on. "But we're on to you and it's you who's been playing into our hands all along."

Aris's silence thundered in her ears.

Damon's derision rose. "But we're reasonable people. And you *are* Alex's biological father, regretfully. So for his sake, we're prepared to tolerate you entering our family. We might even be persuaded to let you back into the contract."

So they were rubbing it in, but knew they couldn't be enemies for her and Alex's sake, and they were prepared to negotiate?

She didn't *want* them to negotiate. She wouldn't have Aris treated with suspicion and condescension. These brothers of hers *would* offer him humble apologies and request the privilege of working with him. She'd see to it.

But Lysandros had more. "So, Sarantos, here's the deal. If you want this contract, we demand an incentive, collateral in case you turn on us again. Which we're certain you will if you can."

Nikolas moved closer to Aris, as if going for the kill. Then he made his thrust. "Half of your fortune and holdings, in Selene's and Alex's names, up front."

She'd never known she could experience or withstand anything as brutal as the fury that exploded inside her in that moment.

Fueling it was fear—that they were causing irreparable damage to her and Aris's relationship.

And she found her voice at last, growled, "Listen you posturing, macho morons…" Three pairs of eyes jerked to her in shock. She'd never talked to her older brothers anywhere near that coldly or rudely. "You're making bigger asses of yourselves and making a bigger mess of everything with every word out of your stupid mouths. Do yourselves a favor, and butt out. And *stay* out."

But she could feel them shrugging off her fury and focusing back on their mission. Aris.

She had one option left. To ask Aris to leave. There was everything to lose by confronting her testosterone-drunk brothers now. She'd talk them away from their warpath when he was gone, taking the cockfighting element out of the equation.

She turned to Aris, and got a harsher blow than any she'd sustained so far. He was looking at her as if *she* were the enemy.

This time, the expression didn't evaporate.

He released her from it only to transfer it to Nikolas, who was glaring back with as much abhorrence.

Nikolas cocked an eyebrow. "Do we have a deal, Sarantos?"

And Aris finally spoke, in a cold-as-the-grave snarl, "We certainly don't, Louvardis."

Damon barked a mirthless laugh. "Why am I not surprised? But phew, thanks. I was almost afraid you'd take the deal, then force us to waste more time on you as you try to weasel out of it."

"That's that, then, Sarantos," Lysandros said. "Now get the hell out. You've lost. Take it like a man. Though, considering how low you've gone this time…" He looked at Selene then back to Aris with a grimace of disgust. "I doubt you are one."

Aris took two steps back from her so he had them all in the trajectory of his arctic animosity before his pitiless calm froze her solid. "With all your talk about being on to me, you clearly have no idea who you're dealing with. If you had a trace of your father's intellect, you would have accepted *any* way out I offered you. But you went and tried to play dirty, you pampered, privileged-from-birth little boys. Now let a master show you how it's done. I'll make you beg me to take everything you've stolen from me and far, far more by the time I'm done with you all."

Then he turned on his heel.

She hurtled after him. *"Aris."*

He put his hand on top of the trembling hand that caught his arm. Then he undid its convulsive grip as if he was unhooking a slimy, poisonous creature from his flesh.

With one last annihilating look that told her he *was* lumping her in with her brothers, declaring war on her, too, he turned and strode out.

She watched him walk away. And knew.

He was walking out of her life.

The life he'd never truly entered, or wanted to be in, if he could turn on her, walk away that easily.

Nikolas's consoling hand on her shoulder felt like a red-hot brand. "I'm sorry it had to end this way, but the sooner you realize you've been played by someone who'll stop at literally nothing to get what he wants, the sooner you'll get over it."

Lysandros's bolstering touch on her back felt like a whip on her aching flesh. "We know it hurts now, but it's for the best, sis. He would have picked your bones and spit you out sooner or later. We just forced him to do it now before he damaged you for life and did the same to Alex."

Damon, her closest brother, and clearly the most disturbed by her role in the whole thing, shook his head in disbelief. "I don't know how you fell for his act, how you—"

"*Stop* it."

She couldn't bear it. Being touched. Hearing anything. Logic, consolation, blame, promises that she'd get over it. She didn't *want* to get over it. Didn't want anything. Didn't want to breathe. To be. To…to… And she wailed, "Leave me alone. Just *leave* me."

She sank into turmoil after that, barely seeing their faces darken with concern, or hearing their protests that she shouldn't be alone now. Then she saw or heard nothing but the bloodred cacophonous landscape of her own shock and grief.

Her brothers' accusations, the corroboration of Aris's silence, then his threats, his desertion, hacked at her, gored her mind as they rewrote all their time together, his every word and look and touch with their macabre interpretation.

She knew hearts didn't get crushed. Not by emotions.

She didn't care what she knew. Hers was. Ruptured, mangled into a bleeding mess inside her.

It had all been a lie.

* * *

It took her two days to come out of her haze of misery.

She did only to call her brothers. They came to her condo one after the other, and she saw her condition reflected in the horrified looks in their eyes.

The moment they were all there, she started. "I want you all to do something you'd never do of your own accord. But if you care about me and Alex, you'll do it."

Damon groaned, "*Theos,* Sel. We only did what we did because we care, because we want you to be happy."

"Too late for that." She heard her lifeless voice, saw its effect in their pained grimaces. "But you can help give me closure. Please, let Aris…" She paused, swallowed. She couldn't call him anything else yet. "Let him back into the contract."

They exchanged an uncomfortable look. Then Nikolas sighed. "Believe me, Selene, if we could pay for your peace of mind with that, we would have considered it a very cheap price."

"You mean you won't?" she choked.

Lysandros shook his head. "We *can't.* Sarantos already carried out his threat. He wrested the contract out of our hands. He's now the builder, and he'll decide who the out-fitters will be."

Damon exhaled. "We're damned if we know how he managed that."

But she suddenly did. In the last days, when he'd seemed to open up to her, she'd told him everything, too. Among the confidences had been information she realized now that he could use—and evidently *had* used—against Louvardis.

So this was her confirmation that his manipulations and exploitations knew no bounds.

Only one thing was left inside her now. Fear. For Alex.

What would the monster she now knew Aristedes Sarantos to be do to get his son?

Even if Alex had started out being the pawn Aris had played to checkmate her and her brothers, she had no doubt he wanted him now. From the depths of his fathomless abyss of a heart.

But then, she'd been certain he'd wanted her.

She hoped she was wrong about his feelings for Alex, too.

Or she'd have to fight the devil for her son.

The next day, she dragged herself into her office.

She had to prepare a battle plan in case Aris decided to fight her for Alex. So far, she could see no way to block him if he decided to play dirty to get Alex.

She jerked as her door burst open. Her PA's mortified voice blurted out in the background.

"I tried to stop him, but—"

Everything tapered off into a vacuum.

A vacuum that Aris filled.

So it's true, she thought. She felt nothing. Not shock, not anger, not pain. Nothing. He *had* finished her.

He closed in on her like a stalking tiger, pinning her with the power of his inescapable intent and her dreadful fascination.

He came around her desk like he had that day a lifetime ago, slapped the dossier he was holding onto its surface. He glared at her, his face a mask of fierceness. That face that had filled her fantasies, commandeered her emotions since she was old enough to realize her femininity. That face she'd always felt was carved of power and nobility, but that camouflaged his cruelty and deceit.

"I think congratulations on your sweeping victory are in or—"

Her words backlashed in her chest. Aris swooped down, clamped her arms in a convulsive grip, hauled her out of her seat, brought her slamming against him, again like that day from another life.

After a moment of paralysis, she squirmed in a silent struggle as he held her captive.

Suddenly the mask of his intensity cracked, contorted with an array of what so uncannily simulated distraught emotions.

She began to struggle for real now, desperate not to be snared in his heartless manipulations again.

"Let me *go*," she cried out, a trapped beast's last desperate protest before it was devoured.

"Never." His growl consumed her in its finality and inescapability as his lips crashed down on hers.

Ten

Aris was kissing her.

Kissing her as if she were the air he'd been suffocating for, as if he'd absorb her into a being that had been disintegrating without her.

No. She wouldn't let him draw her into the illusion again. She wouldn't let the heart and body that were starving for him tell her what they were dying to believe.

She struggled harder, against her own overriding needs, the clamor of everything in her urging her to surrender, take whatever she could have with him, of him, on any terms.

He at last wrenched his lips away, leaving hers stinging and swollen and bereft. She almost pulled his head back down, sealed their lips again, and her fate.

The moment of madness sheared past, and she had to hurt herself now, badly, to prevent worse future injuries.

"What will you do now?" she moaned. "Take me, and keep me, against my will?"

His eyes stormed as they bored into hers. "It won't be against your will. Whatever else you feel or don't feel for me, you want *this*." He pressed her against the wall, lifting her off the floor and into his power, his hunger hard and imprinting every inch of her. "You want *me*, Selene."

She jerked her head away as he swooped down again to claim her lips, had the heat and insistence of his hunger trail a path of devastation down her cheek and jaw and neck instead.

And she sobbed. "It doesn't matter anymore if I do. It's over. You have your victory. And you'll have to be content with it, because you won't have more from me."

His feverish lips stopped feeding at her pulse, stilled. Then he set her back on her feet.

Another agonizing moment pounded by as he stood there, his body curved over hers, a prison of passion she almost begged with every breath to never escape. Then, before she broke, succumbed, uttered the plea for a life sentence, he stepped away.

He brooded down at her until she could no longer bear the abrasion of his will-bending influence.

"Why are you here?" she choked. "You didn't think you'd pick up from where you stormed off three days ago, did you?"

"I'm here to tell you I don't care."

She lurched as if he'd slapped her.

Would even he be so cruel as to come here, kiss her within an inch of her sanity, only to tell her he didn't care about her?

And he was piling confusion on misery. "I don't care what happened. I don't care if your brothers pressured you, or if you felt you owed it to your father's memory to see through his will."

She shook her head. "What the hell are you talking about?"

"I'm talking about how your brothers eliminated me from the contract using information only I knew. Until I told it to you."

Everything went still again. Then she jerked with the slam of comprehension.

That was why he'd looked at her so strangely when he'd gotten that phone call, the one informing him of her brothers' coup. He...he... "You thought I *gave* them information?"

His eyes said he did.

Suddenly the intensity of his gaze wavered, as the certainty there shook. "They may have tricked you into inadvertently revealing that privileged info." Then fractured. "Or they may actually be so good that they worked it out on their own."

"So what will it be?" she rasped. "Which version will you sanction?"

He stared at her for one more moment, then he squeezed his eyes shut, his face clenching as if with severe pain. He opened his eyes again, bruised and defeated now that the anger and outrage was drained from their depths. "You had nothing to do with it."

"Why, thank you! So good to be exonerated with a word from you. Just like I was accused, tried and sentenced without a word."

"I didn't want to believe it. Even when all evidence supported it. Then Alex was injured. It almost shattered me when I thought I'd lose him, and you. I might have looked strong as I took care of the crisis, but inside I was pulverized. I realized then that I've come to depend on you, on both of you, for my very breath. Then you suddenly wanted to go back, and it shook me further. I was at my weakest when your brothers confronted me with their victory and insinuations and demands and their every word seemed to validate my fears. I admit I let my worst suspicions take control of me for a while."

"For a *while?* They were in control till moments ago!"

"But it took only the proof of looking into your eyes for me to know I was wrong. But even when I thought I was right, thought you never really loved me, I still didn't care. I still wanted you."

"I'm supposed to be happy about this, that you'd take me warts and all? You believed the worst about me, passed judgment without giving me a moment's benefit of the doubt. Then you turned and committed the same crime you thought me guilty of! You took the privileged info *I* so trustingly—so stupidly—shared with you and snatched control of the contracts from my family."

"I *didn't.*"

His roar speared through her with its passion. And she had to believe he hadn't. That soothed a measure of her heartache, but that he'd mistrusted her so totally... The scope and implications of that knowledge expanded inside her like the shock waves of a nuclear explosion, razing everything in its path.

He watched her with what looked like dread taking a firmer grip of his features by the second. Then he groaned, "I *am* the best at what I do—I can work my way around anything, in business. But in personal relationships it seems I'm almost clueless." He clutched his hair as if he'd start tearing it out any second. "I took control of the contract only to show you that I can have my so-called victory if I want it, but that *nothing* means anything to me if I don't have you and Alex, too."

"You don't deserve us," she cried. "I hope absolute power will be as cold and cruel a companion to you as you are, for the rest of your isolated life. Yes, Aris, I will fight you to my last breath for Alex. I won't let someone as paranoid and self-serving as you are be his father. I'm only thankful he's too young to remember you and won't grow up knowing he has such a monster for a father."

He held out hands as if begging, *Stop, enough.*

Then he motioned toward the dossier he'd dropped on her desk. "This is what I came to give you—my proof that even when I thought you chose your family over me, I never chose anything over you. This contains all the documents giving control of the contract back to your brothers."

She stared from him to the dossier, her thoughts burning up.

Then she heard her ragged taunt. "This could be your newest ploy to have your cake and eat it, too. Being the best at what you do, you calculated that you might have won the battle with Louvardis, but that the war, now that it's really personal, would escalate to levels even you might not withstand. So you decided it's wiser to throw the contract back as a goodwill gesture, and to keep me and Alex as your permanent insurance."

"Selene, I beg you…don't."

"Don't what? Don't give you a taste of your own paranoia? Don't tell you what you did to me, to Alex, when you walked out on us, thinking only of yourself? Alex cried himself to sleep every night since—he expected you to be there, and you weren't, and I couldn't tell him why you weren't, couldn't assure him you'd ever be back, or if you were, that it wouldn't be even worse for both of us. You are your father's son, after all."

"*No.* Selene, no. I am *nothing* like my father."

"But that's what you always believed. Turns out, you were right." She needed to expend that last surge of hurt. Only feeling his would assuage hers now. Then they'd be even. They could start anew then. "Maybe your father didn't leave his family because he didn't care for you, but like *you* said, because he loved you too much and couldn't handle 'depending on you for his very breath.'"

"I swear this was not—"

"Don't swear. You can always find another reason to walk away that is perfectly acceptable to you, and I can't risk going through this again, if not for myself, then for Alex. He needs a whole and healthy mother, not a mass of anxiety and misery."

He staggered back a step, his shoulders slumping. "I will bring you proof that this will never happen. And I will prove to you that we were both wrong about me. I'm not my father's son, Selene. I'm not a twisted, unfeeling, selfish deserter. Don't give up on me, *agape mou*. Don't let me out of your heart yet."

She gave him a wary nod, her heart starting to expand inside her with resurging belief.

Just when she thought he'd take her in his arms again, knew that she'd dissolve there and sob out her love and surrender in his embrace, tell him she wanted no proofs, forgave him, he gave her a solemn nod, as if he'd received a binding oath, and turned away.

She stared after him as he walked out of her office looking like a warrior demigod embarking on a mission with impossible odds and ultimate dangers, determined to not come back without his trophy.

She didn't hear from Aris again for four days.

The doubt demons started coming back to whisper in her ear, getting louder with each passing empty, lonely, gnawing moment.

What if he'd ended up thinking she and Alex weren't worth the price of having someone love and depend on him for the rest of his life? What if he was saving himself the endless complications of intimacy, going back to his comfortably numb life of isolation?

She couldn't believe that. But doubt was malignant, found her weak in his absence and ate at her.

On the fifth day, she was putting Alex down for his afternoon nap when her cell phone rang.

Damon started talking without preliminaries as usual. "I'm double-parked in front of your building. Come right down."

Before she could say anything, he hung up.

Within minutes, she'd secured the sleeping Alex in his car seat and hopped in beside Damon. She bombarded him with questions, and he said only that he didn't know for sure what was going on. But they'd all know soon.

The next half hour was consumed in speculation and dread and heart-bursting anticipation. She had no doubt this was about Aris. But what about him? Was he waiting for them wherever Damon was taking her? With his "proof"? What could it possibly be this time?

It turned out they were heading to the Louvardis mansion where Nikolas had come back to live, if only until they decided what to do about it.

Once inside, Damon rushed her to the waiting room of their father's old office, now Nikolas's.

"Wait here, and don't move under any condition, okay?" She opened her mouth and his finger on her lips silenced whatever exclamation hadn't formed yet in her mind. "Just listen. Whatever this turns out to be, it should be interesting."

She put Alex on his blanket on the floor then collapsed on the nearest couch to the door Damon had left ajar.

The next second, even though she was half expecting it,

she almost jumped out of her skin when she heard Aris's voice.

It had a world of frustration and haggardness in its beloved depths. "Am I allowed to speak now that the full tribune is assembled?"

"You may say your piece," Damon mocked. "Make it short, though, Sarantos. We don't have all day."

"It won't be short, Louvardis. So pour yourself a drink and endure it." Aris exhaled, then began to talk.

"I was the firstborn of my parents. My mother was seventeen when she had me, hadn't had any measure of formal education, married the man who got her pregnant. He was four years older, a charmer who never held a job for longer than a couple months. He drifted in and out of our lives, each time coming back to add another child to his brood, another burden on my mother's shoulders, before disappearing. He always came back swearing his love, offering sob stories about how hard life was, when he had the easiest life of us all. By the time I was seven, I was doing everything for the household that he should have been doing. By twelve I had to leave school and work four jobs to barely make ends meet. My father disappeared from our lives completely before my youngest sister, Caliope, was born.

"I grew up despising the emotions that had led my mother to destroy her life, that my father claimed to have for the wife and children he blighted with his existence. I swore I'd never feel any of those emotions or inflict them on others. They were the ultimate waste of potential and life, and I didn't have a place for them as I faced the world alone and fended for my whole family. I wouldn't let any weakness, as I saw love and partiality induce in others, infect me, wouldn't let any softness or irrationality get into the way of getting things done.

"Soon I believed I *couldn't* feel, ended up believing that I was like my father, incapable of feeling anything for anyone. But instead of pretending otherwise and exploiting others in the name of love, I pulled away from everyone for fear of hurting those close to me. I gave them the only things I believed to be real and of importance—financial security and the support only I, with my growing power, could provide."

He fell silent. After a moment, Nikolas sighed. "Is this lesson in Sarantos history going anywhere?"

"I'll fast-forward to another era," Aris said. "When your family first crashed into my life. I remember that first day like it was hours ago. And, *Theos,* how I envied you all your father. I wanted to impress him with everything in me. But I ended up making him despise me instead."

"He didn't despise you, Sarantos." That was Lysandros, exhaling heavily. "It's probably the main reason *we* did. He admired the hell out of you, always pointed to you when he was chastising us. 'See how Sarantos dealt with this?', 'Sarantos wouldn't have been so stupid!', 'Why can't you be more like Sarantos?' was all we heard for years."

That was news to Selene. It was apparently shocking to Aris, as well. *"Theos!"* he exclaimed. "If he felt that way, then...*why?*"

Nikolas was the one to answer. "I didn't know the answer to that until I read his diaries. He felt you becoming more detached and ruthless as the years went by. He felt he was sort of your surrogate father, thought it was his role to keep you in check, to try to steer you away from the abyss of leaving your humanity totally behind. And while we were totally in the dark about it, he was also aware of Selene's attraction to you, thought he should shape you up into a man he could accept for his daughter."

So her father had known. He'd never intimated that he did.

Oh, Daddy, why did you never tell me?

Nikolas's next words cut short the surge of heartache. "He was also aware of your attraction to her, even if you didn't realize it yourself."

Then her father didn't know everything. Aris hadn't been attracted to her in the past.

Aris answered and demolished that belief. "Oh, I realized it. I wanted Selene from the first day I saw her. But I thought Hektor would never accept me. That *she* would never accept me. So I acted as the businessman who never bids on a hundred-percent losing proposition and stayed away.

"Then a miracle happened, and she reached out to me. But when she walked away, it was the easiest thing in the world for me to assume she thought she'd made a mistake. I left thinking I would never have another chance with her. But I came back, and realized I've been living in hope of this second chance. This time I demanded one, and she rejected me so hard I'm still aching. *Then* I discovered she'd given me Alex…. Yes, I am not so convoluted as you think me. I didn't know about Alex, because I didn't keep tabs on Selene. I couldn't…bear knowing that she'd moved on, found someone to love. But when I knew she hadn't…and then I saw Alex…I was scared as I've never been before in my life. Because another chance with Selene became a matter of life or death. And she wasn't giving me one—in fact, she held up a mirror to me, showing me the worst that I feared about myself.

"But then another miracle happened. She gave me a chance, and this time, she didn't only want me, she…*got* me, got the best out of me, made me realize I'm not the cold calculating man we all thought me to be. I can barely breathe with the magnitude of my love for her and Alex sometimes. I have no life without them now. I'd rather die than not have her, them, with me.

"But the real miracle was that she loved me back. And I didn't understand how I could deserve to be loved by her. So when I heard the news about your coup with the contract, it made more sense to think that she didn't love me as much as I did her, but chose to help her family against me."

"You thought she gave us the info to preempt you?" Damon snarled. "And you say you love her?"

Lysandros said with the same ferocity, "Yeah, talk is cheap, Sarantos. You love her, you'd give your life for her, but you don't have a smidgen of belief in her."

"I didn't have it in *myself*. It was my own insecurity, not a lack of belief in her. But I had my insecurity under control—until Alex's accident almost uprooted my sanity, and then you surrounded me in her condo, lashed me with your triumph and with more insinuations that led me to believe my worst suspicions were true. I went berserk with pain and walked out.

"As soon as I left, I wanted to rush back, beg for anything she'd give me, even if her family would always come first. But I knew I had to prove that the contract and anything else from the past didn't come into what we shared. So I had to take the contract back so I could give it to her, to refute your accusations."

"So, you basically want to have your cake and eat it, too," Damon argued.

"Yeah, who do you think you're fooling, Sarantos?" Nikolas muttered. "So the contract *is* big, but not big enough for you."

"And when we asked for something that is big," Lysandros added, "you refused."

"You're damn right I refused," Aris growled back, painting her a mental image of him and her brothers facing off like a pack of wolves, fangs bared. "*You* don't get to put a price on what Selene, what Alex…what my *family* is worth to me."

"So your refusal stands, huh?" Damon scoffed. "I figured it would. We're talking more than twelve billion, after all."

"Half my fortune is more than *twenty-four* billion, Louvardis," Aris snapped. "And no, you can't have that. I'll make my own offer."

Selene's heart constricted. She couldn't bear it if he started some cold negotiation to lower the price.

Nikolas exhaled heavily. "Keep your offers, Sarantos. We want nothing from you. And Selene and Alex will sure as hell never need anything from you. We'll make sure of that."

"Guess you're not as shrewd as we thought," Lysandros mused. "You didn't project that you stood to gain so much more if you made that investment in our goodwill and Selene's support."

"That's right, Sarantos," Damon taunted. "It was a test. You would have passed it, you idiot, if you'd agreed to it verbally. We would never have pushed for application. Now, anything you say or offer means nothing. Worse than nothing."

Selene felt her heart splinter in her chest.

How would Aris answer them? What would he say?

The next moment he did. "I would have been an idiot if I'd *taken* your offer. As I said, in the matter of proving my commitment to Selene and Alex, I don't bow to demands, but I, and only I, will submit my own bid. And here it is."

She heard Nikolas's grunt as something solid and padded seemed to land against his flesh.

In a moment she heard the sound of a briefcase being opened, then papers being passed around.

At last, Nikolas exclaimed, "You...*madman*. You *mean* this?"

Damon sounded as stunned. "Okay, where's the catch? I can't find it, but it *has* to be here."

Lysandros chimed in, just as dazed. "Point it out and get done with it, Sarantos!"

"No catch," Aris said calmly. "I think half my empire for Selene and Alex is an insult. They're everything to me, and they deserve *all* of it. And everything I acquire from here on. You can now shred it all apart if you so wish, for all I care."

Nikolas let out a resounding guffaw. "You *are* insane."

"I didn't even know you owned most of the Di Giordanos stock," Lysandros said, a deep tinge of admiration entering his stunned voice. "And PrimeTech. And Futures Inc. Father *was* right. You are well on the way to global domination."

Damon whistled. "And you're *really* giving it all to Selene."

"It's nowhere near her worth," Aris said. "All my assets are just a token. She owns all of me, and I'm offering her my *life,* under any terms she, and you, as her brothers and protectors, wish to impose. I botched my first two chances with her. I will offer anything if she will agree to give me a third, and final, chance. I only truly lived during those weeks with her and Alex. Will you help me have that chance to live again?"

And the paralysis that had deepened with each incredible word out of Aris's mouth shattered. She rocketed into the room.

He seemed taken aback at the sight of her. "Selene..." His rise to his feet was impeded by the same emotions ricocheting inside her, his eyes feverish on her face, making her feel treasured, needed, loved to her last cell. "I came to—"

She couldn't bear for him to say one more word, to surrender any further. "I heard *everything.*"

His lips twitched, a tidal wave of heat entering his gaze. "Eavesdropping, *agape mou?*"

Before she could say anything more, a newly toddling Alex spilled into the room, fell flat on his face, came up on his hands and knees and ate up the distance between himself and Aris in an accelerated crawl, ending up launching himself at his father.

Aris groaned, his reddened eyes tearing as he swooped down and picked up Alex, as if he were diving after the heart that had spilled out of his chest.

Tears were now a constant stream flooding down Selene's cheeks. Her heart almost burst with needing to throw herself into his arms and beg him to never let her go again. But she had to give him this moment with Alex first.

Suddenly, Aris kneeled before her, Alex and all. "Will you agree to marry me...again?"

She rained tears of joy on his face. "Oh, my love, I will agree to anything and everything you ask, for as long as I live."

Alex was gazing up at her with the same expectation, shrieked with glee as her tears splashed on his gleaming cheeks. She swooped down on the two people who formed the soul that existed outside her body, hugged them with all her strength, showered them with her love and gratitude.

Aris gathered her with Alex between them, rocked on his heels as he broke out litanies of love and worship and relief. "My love for you and Alex has made me the person I was supposed to be before life forced me to steel my heart and hide inside my isolation. But don't take my word for it. You can keep me on probation for as long as you see fit. In fact, I demand it."

She squeezed him tighter, her tears running faster. "For

all you put me through, for making me love you so much that I'm empty and lost without you, you deserve a few decades or so of probation."

"I'll outbid you," he groaned against her cheeks, her eyes, her lips. "A life sentence, and beyond."

A cough brought them out of their surrender to the bliss of finding each other again. They all turned to her brothers.

Lysandros was gaping at them. "All right. This is… disturbing."

Damon snorted. "Tell me about it. This love thing is now officially *the* scariest sickness I've ever seen. Seeing Sarantos of all men in this condition is definitely creepy."

Nikolas nodded his emphatic agreement. "It's enough to make me run the other way the next time I see an attractive woman. I *don't* want this to happen to me."

Damon shuddered dramatically. "You and me both."

Aris smirked at her brothers. "You better get down on your knees and pray this, or even a fraction of this, happens to you. It would be the one thing that would make your life worth anything."

Her brothers rolled their eyes as if on cue.

Damon then looked at Selene in open amazement. "And to think our kid sister has the power to tame the world's biggest monster, have him on a leash purring and rolling over this way."

Lysandros nodded. "Guess we'll have to take her really seriously from now on."

Nikolas eyed Aris in consideration. "What worries *me* now is how the hell we'll adjust from considering you public enemy number one to brother-in-law."

"It'll be a real challenge…Aris," Lysandros said, letting the name slide off his tongue, clearly not liking its taste.

"Don't." Aris winced. "You keep on calling me Sarantos.

Or don't call me anything, if you prefer. But you *don't* get to call me Aris. That's Selene's and only Selene's."

"Fine, what's-your-name." Damon laughed. "I'll be watching you."

Lysandros added, "Ditto. I think it'll take another decade for me to wipe from my mind what the past ten years of you engraved in it."

At that point, Apollo, whom she'd left at the mansion while she and Alex were away and hadn't yet taken back home, scampered into the office and made a beeline for them, including Aris in his warmest welcome of his family.

Damon cracked a booming laugh. "All right. Maybe we don't need to keep a close eye on you after all, Sarantos. Granted, you're an uncanny enough businessman that your 'proofs' might ultimately mean nothing, while Selene loving you is of no consequence in my eyes, since she's a woman and can be fooled. But Alex's love for you gave me pause. Now Apollo seals the deal. A cat is the ultimate litmus test. If he thinks you're okay, and evidently can't get enough of you, you can't be all bad."

Nikolas and Lysandros laughed. Selene laughed, too, a new rush of relief and elation surging through her.

Even if all the heartache she'd suffered hadn't led to uniting with Aris, it would have been worth it to see her brothers at ease together for once. Their love for her and their stand against what they'd perceived as a common enemy had made them put their differences aside. She could only hope, now that those unifying factors were no more, they wouldn't become estranged again.

But for now, she couldn't think about that. She only had one thing on her mind. Aris.

Leaving Alex and Apollo with her brothers, she grabbed

Aris and his "briefcase of sacrifice" and ran them up to her old room.

The moment they entered, she pushed him against the door, climbed him, owned every inch of flesh she could reach with lips and hands made aggressive in her yearning.

He surrendered to her, letting her devour him, brand him, own him, a litany of bass groans rumbling from his depths. *"S'aghapo, Selene, s'aphapo, apape mou."*

And she sobbed, "And I love you, my love, my Aris. I've loved you forever."

He growled, took over.

He took her to her bed, threw them both down on it in a tangle of entwining limbs and lips and lingering sighs.

She didn't know how or when, but he had them both naked, their flesh mingling, straining against each other with the fevered need to merge, to never part again.

Suddenly, before he could complete their union, she pushed him away.

He fell to his back. His shock became fierce protest as he realized why she'd left him.

While he was unable to move with the blow of aborted arousal, she jumped off the bed, zoomed to the briefcase, extracted the documents and ran to her paper shredder.

His protests died as the machine devoured the last of the papers. He approached her, her demigod who'd brought her back proof of his worthiness of forever.

A challenge was tingeing the love blazing on his face. "That's just one copy of endless ones I can order made."

She kissed him silent. "*I* order you not to make any." He enfolded her in his arms and she whispered against his adoring lips, "All I'll ever need is for you to be mine, to let me be yours."

"I am, all yours. Always have been, always will be, for

as long as I live." He swung her up in his arms, fused her against his heat and hunger, murmured hungrily against her lips, "Now, about being mine…"

* * * * *

No one does power and passion like Olivia Gates!
Watch for her next emotional and seductive novel,
TO TOUCH A SHEIK,
the conclusion of
THE PRIDE OF ZOHAYD *trilogy.*
Only from Harlequin Desire!

COMING NEXT MONTH

Available May 10, 2011

#2083 KING'S MILLION-DOLLAR SECRET
Maureen Child
Kings of California

#2084 EXPOSED: HER UNDERCOVER MILLIONAIRE
Michelle Celmer
The Takeover

#2085 SECRET SON, CONVENIENT WIFE
Maxine Sullivan
Billionaires and Babies

#2086 TEXAS-SIZED TEMPTATION
Sara Orwig
Stetsons & CEOs

#2087 DANTE'S HONOR-BOUND HUSBAND
Day Leclaire
The Dante Legacy

#2088 CARRYING THE RANCHER'S HEIR
Charlene Sands

HDCNM0411

*With an evil force hell-bent on destruction,
two enemies must unite to find a truth that turns
all-too-personal when passions collide.*

*Enjoy a sneak peek in Jenna Kernan's next installment
in her original* TRACKER *series,* GHOST STALKER,
available in May, only from Harlequin Nocturne.

"Who are you?" he snarled.

Jessie lifted her chin. "Your better."

His smile was cold. "Such arrogance could only come from a Niyanoka."

She nodded. "Why are you here?"

"I don't know." He glanced about her room. "I asked the birds to take me to a healer."

"And they have done so. Is that *all* you asked?"

"No. To lead them away from my friends." His eyes fluttered and she saw them roll over white.

Jessie straightened, preparing to flee, but he roused himself and mastered the momentary weakness. His eyes snapped open, locking on her.

Her heart hammered as she inched back.

"Lead who away?" she whispered, suddenly afraid of the answer.

"The ghosts. Nagi sent them to attack me so I would bring them to her."

The wolf must be deranged because Nagi did not send ghosts to attack living creatures. He captured the evil ones after their death if they refused to walk the Way of Souls, forcing them to face judgment.

"Her? The healer you seek is also female?"

"Michaela. She's Niyanoka, like you. The last Seer of Souls and Nagi wants her dead."

Jessie fell back to her seat on the carpet as the possibility of this ricocheted in her brain. Could it be true?

"Why should I believe you?" But she knew why. His black aura, the part that said he had been touched by death. Only a ghost could do that. But it made no sense.

Why would Nagi hunt one of her people and why would a Skinwalker want to protect her? She had been trained from birth to hate the Skinwalkers, to consider them a threat.

His intent blue eyes pinned her. Jessie felt her mouth go dry as she considered the impossible. Could the trickster be speaking the truth? Great Mystery, what evil was this?

She stared in astonishment. There was only one way to find her answers. But she had never even met a Skinwalker before and so did not even know if they dreamed.

But if he dreamed, she would have her chance to learn the truth.

Look for GHOST STALKER by Jenna Kernan,
available May only from Harlequin Nocturne,
wherever books and ebooks are sold.

HNEXP0511

SAME GREAT STORIES AND AUTHORS!

Starting April 2011,
Silhouette Desire will become
Harlequin Desire, but rest assured
that this series will continue to be
the ultimate destination for Powerful,
Passionate and Provocative Romance
with the same great authors that
you've come to know and love!

♦ Harlequin®

Desire

ALWAYS POWERFUL, PASSIONATE
AND PROVOCATIVE

SDHARLEQUIN11